THE MEETING TREE

by

LENA TASI

BRASS INK

United States

"Founded on principles so pure, the order of Chivalry could not, in the abstract at least, but occasion a pleasing, though a romantic development of the energies of human nature. But as, in actual practice, every institution becomes deteriorated and degraded, we have too much occasion to remark, that the devotion of the knights often degenerated into superstition,— their love into licentiousness,—their spirit of loyalty or of freedom into tyranny and turmoil,—their generosity and gallantry into hare-brained madness and absurdity."
—Sir Walter Scott
"An Essay on Chivalry"
1818

NEVADA

A few generations from now

Adla wasn't supposed to go up to the roof for any reason until full dark. Even though she almost always tried to sneak out just early enough to catch the late sun's deep gold on the leaves of her grandfather's olive trees, she was too early for it tonight.

The light was still white, revealing the bigness of the desert beyond town, the many shapes and sizes of plants growing out of the sand, and the small clearing between the edge of town and Adla's grandfather's trees where the plants seemed not to grow. Distant car engines hummed—it wasn't curfew, yet—and people were still out walking in the streets and alleyways, their deep voices carrying up to the roof.

"Hi, Mr. Jarvis." This voice was higher, and very close.

"Reuben," Adla's father said below. "Out kind of late, aren't you?"

Adla walked in a crouch to the west-facing wall. She gripped the edge and peered over it into the alley.

"I'm eleven." Reuben's hands were in the front pockets of his loose green shorts, and his black t-shirt was neatly tucked in.

"You are, are you?"

"And my dad's out of town, too."

"Isn't your mother home?"

"Well, sure. Where else would she be?"

"Yes," Abe said. "I…I suppose you're right."

"Anyway, I'm pretty hungry, so I guess I better go in. Night, Mr. Jarvis."

"Good night, Reuben."

Reuben unlocked the door to his house across the alley and went inside.

The men started straightening their merchandise for end-of-day lockup. Most of the booths were red, green, or brown, but Abe's was the same cheerful yellow as the daily sheet the guards tacked to people's doors. In a few minutes, Abe and all of the other men would roll down their front shutters, lock them with padlocks, and go into their houses, bringing those yellow sheets with them if they hadn't been brought in, already.

Abe touched up his stacks of folded linen shirts and white, pink, and gray caftans, gliding his hand in a straight downward line in the dark spaces between the stacks to feel for unevenness. Adla backed away from the roof's edge so he wouldn't look up and see her and call her down to help, taking away her chance to practice.

It still wasn't dark, so she sat cross-legged in the middle of the roof listening to the shuttering sounds, the thud of her father closing the door that opened from the alley into their living room, and people's voices fading to nothing. At first stars she stood up, rubbed sand dust off her palms, and sneaked in a bent, careful walk to the edge of the rooftop.

The alley was bare. In the far distance, solar panels reflected moonlight on top of the big houses where rich people lived, and where, Adla's mother liked to say, the only difference was "the size of the enclosure." Closer by, where the homes were small and cheap, squares of amber light marked the windows where people still lived in them. Those abandoned through death or upward movement, and not nearly nice enough to interest even the lowest levels of small-town government, were always dark.

She skipped to the other side and scanned the acres leading to the olive trees. No visible activity. She kicked off her sandals and went to the big cinderblock in the corner, positioned her feet perfectly parallel in front of it like she was supposed to, and made sure to hold that position as she jumped up onto it. Somehow, one foot got caught beneath the other at the top and she fell off sideways, landing on her knee.

"Clumsy!" Ruth whisper-shouted. She was silent clapping from on top of her own house across the alley, her head turning right to left in her warm-up stretch. In daylight her roof was more colorful than Adla's, with lawn chairs made of blue and orange plastic strips and clothes hanging on a line stretching from one corner to the other. Ruth's mom's were the brightest of all the pairs of underwear ever pinned to any rooftop cable. "Did you do warmups?" Ruth was stretching out her arms, one after the other. She'd come closer to the edge and didn't have to whisper so loud.

Adla examined her stinging knee. Bleeding. "Didn't want to."

"But maybe then you wouldn't fall."

Adla pulled her knee close and spit on her thumb. "You fell last week." She wiped at the blood.

"Anyway, you should've rolled, too."

Adla mimicked her, and Ruth laughed into her hands. Then, squinting at Adla in the dim light of streetlamps and the moon, she said, "Wow. Your mom cut your hair really short this time."

There was a faint noise below. Adla listened, but it didn't come again.

Ruth was waving at her.

Adla flung up her hands. *What?*

"You did pigeon toes," she whispered. "I saw it. You have to do it like her, with your toes like this." She demonstrated with her hands held flat, side by side, touching at the thumbs. She got behind one of her lawn chairs and wrapped her arms around its wide back, picked it up, and leaned back with it so the aluminum legs wouldn't drag as she moved it away from the low patio table to make space. "Like this." She planted her feet together, bent her knees, drew her arms back, and jumped, landing almost in the dead center of the table with her feet perfectly parallel.

"I did that," Adla whispered, "but—"

"Watch me land on that crack."

Now there was a dull, metal clanking followed by the rough sliding noise familiar to Adla. It was her father's booth. Voices sounded below, one of them his.

Ruth hopped easily off the table and mouthed, "Parapet," ducking low behind hers so that only her light brown eyes showed. Adla tiptoed to her roof's edge.

Abe was swiping fine sand off painted turquoise letters spelling *Jarvis* while a member of the local government's Institutional Guard, as they were officially called, looked over his merchandise.

"And you make all these?" the guard said.

"My wife." Abe brushed his hand on his pants.

The guard pointed at something, asking to see it up close.

Ruth rolled her eyes big, then shook her head and jabbed her thumb over her shoulder for *Going in.* She whispered, "I can't come out later. I have to do my reading." She made a face.

Adla was behind on hers. She'd have to catch up before bed. She mouthed, "Tomorrow."

Blythe, the red spatula in her hand, was standing at the stove and staring out the window as she often did while standing at the stove, even, at times, when the curtains were closed. "What did you read in your room last night?" she asked, her back to Adla.

Adla pulled at a section of her short hair. "*Home*… Uh…"

"*Homestead Glory*?"

"Ya."

"Yes."

"Yesss."

"Tell me something you remember from *Homestead Glory*."

"Uhh…" Adla pulled at hair from a different part of her head. "Uh…People who…fight…at the teeth of…"

"'Those women,'" her mother recited flatly while scraping at the pan, "'who beat back the claws of temptation'…"

"'Those women who beat back claws of…'"

"'Temptation.'"

"'Temptation…'"

"'…to wander the earth…'"

"'To wander the earth.'"

"'…in a frivolous quest for novelty…'"

"'In a frivolous quest for novelty.'"

"'…are to be honored for their commitment to stand their ground.'"

"'Are to be honored for their…honored for their…'"

"'…commitment to stand their ground.'"

"'Commitment to stand their ground.'"

"Do you know what that means?"

Adla didn't.

"It means you have to stop the jumping, walnut."

Adla curled and uncurled her toes. "But wh—?"

"Adla." Blythe tilted her head back, touching the ends of her long brown hair to the waist of her jeans. She laid the spatula on the spoon rest, turned around, and rested her lower back against the counter. "You can't be up on the roof jumping around where they can see you. Maybe you can do it in—" But Blythe glanced past her, through the kitchen door and into the living room where the sharp-cornered coffee table and end tables were. "Never mind. Why do you have to do it at all?"

Adla scratched her thigh. "I like it."

"Well." Blythe looked at the floor. "Well," she said softer. She sighed. "Adla, you simply don't have time for all that jumping. You have too many lessons as it is that you're not taking seriously. 'Fight at the teeth'?" She laughed in a way that made Adla smile back. "I'll remind you one last time that you're seven. You have to start taking more responsibility." For example, she said, where had Adla been last night when it was time to make dinner? Where was she whenever it was time to fold laundry? "You can't keep hiding when you're needed, and you certainly can't be on the roof where they might—"

Adla opened her mouth.

"Pardon me? Do you have something to say while I'm speaking?"

Adla shook her head.

"No more. The roof. No more, do you understand?"

"But—"

"Adla."

"But I want to be good at it! Me and Ruth—"

"Ruth and I."

"Ruth and I. Me and Ruth have been practicing and if we get really good some day we can be as good as—"

Blythe held up a stopping hand. She opened a drawer under the dish rack and pulled out a thin, stained, hardcover book, a smiling woman in a pink caftan on the front. She opened it and read, "'Women of substance rejoice in their stillness.' What that means, walnut, is that a *good* woman—and in the future, you'll be expected to be a good woman—likes…" She bit her lower lip. "Well, she likes…" She considered the page and shrugged. "The absence of excitement." She went on reading. "'They embrace nature's assigned roles for the sexes, enjoying femininity and denying the temptation to behave in a masculine way.' This means they—*we*—are happy to dress the way we must dress in public, happy to cook and clean, happy to behave like mothers toward our husbands until it's time to have—" She looked at Adla. "Have…Have I explained it well enough? Do you understand?"

Adla nodded.

"What do you understand?"

Adla dropped her head back and blinked at the ceiling. "Uhh… Like, it…I have to help in the kitchen more, and stuff?"

"This is the last part: 'The universe has ordained a peaceful, sedentary'—sedentary means you don't do very much—'existence for women.' " She flapped the book at Adla. "This is serious, my walnut."

But why, Adla wanted to know.

Because it is, her mother said.

But why, Adla still wanted to know. Why couldn't she keep practicing on the roof if she promised to be careful and wipe off the dust before coming inside and not yell or make people look up from the street? She would even do it in her white caftan.

Blythe flung the book into the drawer and slammed it shut. She turned to Adla, then, and at the look on her face went to her and kneeled in front of her. "I'm not mad at you, sweetheart." She pulled out a chair, said, "Sit," and went back to the stove and turned down the burner heat. She called "Abe! Breakfast!" and, out of habit, glanced out the kitchen window.

When she didn't stop looking, Adla climbed up on her chair to look, too.

Abe was standing out front on the other side of their iron gate. A guard stood with him, a rifle slung across the chest of his tactical vest. Most men had that gun, Adla's father had told her the time he'd showed her his own rifle, along with the smaller one, and warned her of all the ways she should never hold or touch a weapon.

Blythe inched to the side until she was out of view should the guard look at the window, then slowly reached for the latch. Adla held her breath while watching her mother ease the window open until hot air pushed in, carrying Abe's and the guard's voices in from the street.

"… reciting this morning's Replenishment?"

"Of course," Abe said. When the guard didn't respond, but simply continued looking at him, he said, "I thought I would do it here."

"Here?" He waved dismissively at the house. "There's no fellowship here. You should be at the lodge." After a moment, he smiled. "Come on. It's a few blocks." He adjusted the strap on his shoulder. "I'll walk with you."

Abe gestured in the direction of the alley and his cart and complained about the extra sand that must have blown in with the winds last night. He needed to shake everything off and refold it so he'd be ready to sell at opening time. Thanks to the diligent guards, he said, pulling the yellow sheet from his front pocket, he had the topic and would ponder on it as deeply as he always did.

The guard was quiet, and then he laughed, patting Abe's shoulder. "You know that sheet's just for preparation, don't you?" He left his hand there. "It's for the women to follow, too, obviously, during their reflections, but without the company of the others at the lodge, you don't experience the benefit of the community." He released Abe's shoulder and put his hand on his own heart. "'Yesterday's triumphs do not give a man permission to rest on his laurels today,'" he recited, and Abe joined him, hand on heart, "'because nothing tempts failure like complacency,'" they finished.

"Ty Victor, immortal in words," the guard said.

"Ty Victor."

Blythe shook her head and muttered, "Ty Victor."

"Who's that?" Adla said.

Blythe put a finger to her lips.

Adla whispered, "Who is it?"

Blythe tiptoed over and said into Adla's ear that he was a writer from years and years ago who wrote a book to help boys become men, but that his book had become too important to the wrong people and those wrong people used it the wrong way.

Adla scratched inside her ear, then rubbed it with her shoulder. "Oh.

Blythe smiled and touched the top of Adla's head. "He's just some dead writer, walnut." She returned to the window, then looked back. "But don't ever repeat that to anyone," she whispered.

Mother and daughter returned their attention outside, where neither man was holding his heart, anymore.

"…get complacent when we don't regularly replenish ourselves with the spirit of our purpose," the guard said. "Don't you agree?"

"Of course," Abe said. "Yes."

The guard rocked back on his tan-sneakered heels and studied Abe from his face to his feet. "You're how old?"

Stiffness overtook Abe's body in a way only his wife and daughter would notice. Adla looked at her mother, but Blythe was very still and listening.

"Thirty-seven."

The guard tilted his head.

Abe raised his arm to the side until it was shy of being straight out from his shoulder. "High as I can get it." He lowered it and told the story of falling off a ladder while hanging a light outside. He was still disappointed about having his service denied, he said, adding a swear word for emphasis.

The guard nodded tiredly, said, "Ah, okay, I see," and followed up with an absent sniff and a look around. His eyes settled on the kitchen window. The sun was coming from the east, shining on the men and leaving the window in the shadows, so it was hard to know what he could see. Blythe didn't move.

"Can he see us?"

Blythe said, "Shh."

"You should stop into the lodge offices," the guard said. "Exciting changes are coming. The old restrictions don't really apply, these days. In any case," he pointed his nose at his weapon, "you could take down twenty before you'd feel anything from the recoil." He squinted at the house. "It's about time we go. You have a wife in there?"

"I do," Abe said. "Yes. I'll just tell her I'm leaving."

"No need. She'll be here when you get back."

Abe said he should probably give the yellow sheet to his wife, but the guard said he could save time by slipping it under the front door, where his wife would surely find it.

Abe walked toward the house without looking at the kitchen window, tucked the yellow sheet under the door, and went back to the sidewalk. The guard started walking. Abe joined him, eyes straight ahead.

Blythe and Adla set up dinner at the living room coffee table, Blythe carrying the plates of chicken and rice and Adla carrying the lighter bowls of salad. Both stopped walking when the lights flickered, then went dark. They continued to the table, hands full, when power returned a few seconds later. When all of the food was down, Blythe tossed a throw pillow at Adla and grabbed another for herself. They dropped them on the floor and sat on them side by side. Chewing filled the silence.

"When's Daddy coming home?" Adla said.

"Not with food in your mouth." Blythe looked at the door to the alley, then back at her plate.

After swallowing, Adla said, "Did he get in trouble?"

"I don't know, walnut."

They fell quiet, focused on their dinners. At a faint noise outside, Blythe looked again at the door. When it didn't open, she checked the clock. It was almost an hour past the time Abe would normally come in after closing the booth for the day, but he hadn't been home to open it. She'd tried to work in the sewing room all that morning and afternoon after he'd left, but she hadn't been able to concentrate and had finished only a shirt and a half. Since he hadn't been in his booth to sell any, there was nothing needing replacing, so it likely didn't matter.

Tick.

Tick.

Tick.

The clock's rhythm matched that of a swaying shadow on the thin curtain, the branches of their rosemary bush backlit by street lamps and framed by the window square. If Abe walked home one way, he would cut through the neighborhood and come down the alley. If he walked home the other way, he would be on the sidewalk, his shadow crossing the curtain before he entered through the kitchen door.

If he walked home.

Her eyes went from the window to the clock to the door. Window, clock, door, window, clock, door. "Adla."

Adla had just lifted her plastic cup for a drink of water and, startled, slammed it hard on the table, splashing water over her plate and hand.

Blythe laughed and used her napkin to mop up. "What daydream did I just shock you out of?" She dried Adla's wet hand.

"I don't know."

"The roof?"

Adla shrugged.

"All right, Adla. You can do it. But inside.—What's that face?"

"But the roof is more fun and Ruth is th—"

"No."

Adla let her fork fall loudly to her plate.

"Or maybe you wouldn't like to do it at all."

Adla's eyes watered and her nose turned red. Blythe told her to get up and wash her face. When Adla returned, Blythe invited her to sit next to her on the couch, then looked at the doors again, and then the clock. She pulled up her feet to sit cross-legged like Adla and tugged her daughter's big toe. "I don't enjoy making you miserable. I'm not telling you not to play on the roof because I like being mean. There's a reason I don't want you up there, just like there's a reason I don't let your hair grow long like mine. Or like Ruth's."

Adla said, "Ruth has to put hers up a lot because she gets hot."

"Short hair is more comfortable in the heat, that's true. But it's also less…How do I say this."

Adla shrugged.

"You're a very pretty little girl, Adla, and that's not a good thing. With shorter hair…The world…The world outside is very different from what you know in here, and it has to do with the roof, and…and this was something your father and I wanted to teach you about together, but…" She put her hands to her face and rubbed up and down. "I need you pay very good attention, okay?"

"'kay."

"It's very, very important."

"'kay."

Many years ago, so far back in time that Adla's Grandpa Jarvis had still been a young man, Blythe said, men and women had already been fighting each other for power for many years, but before all that fighting had begun, men had been the leaders, as they were today. "They had the big, important jobs, and they made most of the money, like now. And, just between us, walnut, they were also responsible for a thriving child sex slave trade, which—"

"Not all men."

Abe was standing in the living room's open door, the dull orange light of the alley behind him. His smile at Adla's "Daddy!" was pained. Small. "Hi, nugget." He closed the door and slipped off his shoes.

Blythe said, "What hap—"

He gave a short shake of his head as he crossed the room to kiss his daughter's head and his wife's cheek. He murmured to Blythe, "Little young for sex slavery talk, don't you think?"

Blythe muttered back, "Tell them that," and, "It just came out. She doesn't know what it means, thank goodness." She grabbed his hand and used it to pull herself off the couch. Abe followed her to the kitchen.

"I thought we were doing this talk together." He pulled a fork from the drawer and scooped rice out of the cooker.

"I thought they killed you."

"Not yet." He considered the rice on his fork, ate it. "How far did you get?"

"Not far." She had wanted to wait, she said, but had known that if the worst had happened, she would have had to explain to Adla why it had happened. "And if I'd waited until I knew for sure that the worst had happened, my love, I'm not sure I could have managed." She stroked the top of his foot with her toes. "So, tell me. What did happen?"

"After." He scooped another heavy forkful and, before putting it in his mouth, said, "Wasn't good." He filled a bowl with what was left in the cooker and followed Blythe back to the living room.

Blythe and Abe sat on the couch with Adla. After making sure she was comfortable and had a glass of water and wasn't still hungry and that there was nothing else that might distract her, they did their best to make her understand her environment by first trying to explain how they'd all arrived there.

So that she would grasp and retain as much as possible, they kept it simple, picking up where Blythe had left off by telling her that girls had started doing better in school than boys.

"They used to go to school together, but not only in the same building, like when you started," Blythe said. "Back then, a boy could sit at the desk right next to yours."

Adla laughed.

"It's true." Blythe explained that the short time Adla had been allowed to attend school, the reason she hadn't had any boys in her classroom was that, back when the boys had gotten mad and scared about girls doing better, they had made sure girls and boys would start learning different things.

"They wanted boys to learn skills that would help them get jobs so they could make money to buy food," Blythe said. "And girls were supposed to learn things that would help them take care of those boys."

Adla scrunched her eyes, then rubbed them.

"Almost done, nugget," Abe said. "You still with us? This is important."

"Ya."

Those boys who hated losing to girls, they said, became adults who then started running the country. They changed the laws one election at a time, making—

"'Elections.' Ha." Abe sipped his water.

—making things worse and worse for girls, Blythe finished.

"Not so great for us menfolk, either." Abe pinched a last bit of rice from his bowl and popped it in his mouth.

They did not tell Adla that less than a year after her grandfather's decision to move his wife and son farther into the desert—along with the others trying to escape what the new government had started calling "an Institution of Chivalry"—its armed force had closed in, bringing with it a newly refined philosophy and system of punishment that boasted *Simpler times, simpler rules*:

Men, considered pragmatic and outward focused, were meant to be workers, fighters, worldly. Women, characterized as emotional and self-focused, were decidedly best suited for homemaking, motherhood, and soothing.

Men were (through no fault of their own, they had argued, but purely as a byproduct of their survival-directed biology) subject to uncontrollable sexual impulses, making them dangerous to women. Women, on the other hand, were pure, but unfortunately they were also (unwittingly, and also as a byproduct of their biology, they had insisted) conniving temptresses who should be kept safe at home from sundown to sunup.

Inspired by the Middle Ages, the Old Testament, and a commitment to order and decisive action, as the government had outlined in one of its many publications, those who did not adhere to the system would be shot by firing squad or stoned to death.

Adla's grandparents had known the risks but had tried, anyway, to find a way to oust some of the leadership, if not overthrow the entire government. Adla already knew her grandparents had died soon after her grandpa had planted his olive trees, but Blythe and Abe had not told her exactly how. When the time came, they had decided, they would take her to the building where the secret meetings had been held before they were discovered, their members—including Adla's grandparents—led at gunpoint to the clearing and shot. They wanted Adla, when she read her grandparents' names on the plaque, to be old enough to understand the significance and the lie of the message engraved above the so-called subversives' names: *May we be forever undeterred in our resolve to protect the weak, the innocent, and the defenseless from the indignities, wrongs, and outrages of the lawless named below.*

Blythe simplified the history, saying, "Your grandparents didn't like the new way things were, so they moved out here with your dad when he was sixteen. But a year later—just after your grandpa Jarvis planted those olive trees, remember?—the bad men came and took over. People tried to fight back, and many of them, including your grandparents, died."

"They didn't die because of cancer?"

"No. Did someone tell you they had cancer?"

Adla shook her head.

"No, walnut," Blythe said.

"Oh."

In any case, Blythe and Abe concluded, that was what had happened, and why they had to live by the rules they lived by. "The rules used to be a little different," Blythe said, "less strict. But they kept changing and changing until they became what they are now. Like…Like the reading we have to do, and the clothes we have to wear outside."

"The white thing?"

"Yes, your white thing. And my pink thing. And when I had to take you out of school after your first month, and you and I had to start staying home even in daytime, that was because of another change in the rules."

Adla blew air at her forehead and rubbed her legs. "But why do I have to listen again because I know all the rules. You and Daddy say all the time to read and all that other stuff."

Blythe shifted, straightening her back and stretching her neck. She looked at Adla, who was stifling a yawn. "You are a girl," Blythe said.

"I kno—"

"What that means to those people out there—and not just the ones in the vests, because it could be any man you see, and even some women—is that you belong in here, in this house, unless you're with your father. Do you understand?"

"I already knowww. I can't go anywhere." She shrugged.

"Yes, but—but you're going to try."

"Nuh-uh."

Abe laughed. "Sure, nugget."

"Adla, this is important." Blythe used a finger to lift Adla's chin and looked directly into her eyes. "We told you all of this because you must know these aren't our rules. They're their rules. Big, scary-government rules. And if they catch you breaking them, my walnut, they'll bring you to a—"

"It will be bad," Abe cleared his throat. "That's good enough. Bedtime."

After putting Adla to bed, Abe explained where he'd been all day, and when he was done, Blythe stood up, blinked, and sat back down. She stood up again and slowly paced the living room. "But…But, work for them how? You sell blankets and the clothes I make. Caftans. Pants. Shirts."

"Yes," Abe said. "And vests."

Blythe stopped. "Yes. Vests. And?"

He waited.

She raised her hands in a question.

"They would like the vests to continue to look like standard, civilian vests," he said, "but with modifications to the lining."

"Different fabric?"

"Now that you mention it, that would be necessary. Yes. Stronger. But also with pockets."

"Inside pockets. Fine."

"Along the width of the waist. Precisely ten of them. So that they wrap," he demonstrated by circling his waist with his hands, "like so."

After a moment, she laughed. "You're not serious."

"'Oh, you don't want your wife to make the vests for us? No problem! How would you like to wear one, instead?'"

"*Suicide* vests? But—But what—" She held up a finger, then tilted her head, listening. "Are you sure she's asleep?"

"She was five minutes ago."

Blythe sat. "*Suicide* vests? Since when? Our government doesn't do that."

"Apparently, they will."

"But—That's—" She shook her head. It wasn't as if the government could be accused of treating citizens humanely, she thought aloud, but at the very least anyone being punished for a crime wasn't surprised. They always knew they had done something against the rules. "But who are they targeting with suicide bombs?" she said. "I don't understand."

"I don't know about targets. But people still don't like the way things are. They still meet. Maybe we're all just not scared enough. Maybe they think it'll be funny to see someone explode. I don't know."

Blythe took one of his hands and held it on her lap. Had Abe wondered who would make the vests if they didn't, she asked, and had he considered suggesting that person make them, instead?

"They were about to take me out to the truck, Bly. I'm not on the guard team. I miss community Replenishment. How committed could I possibly be to their…mightily noble pursuit…if I've never made an effort to bond with them? In the end, I was the one convincing them to buy from us. They were almost done with me."

The light flickered, then went out. They sat in silence in the dark.

Did she and Abe have to pack the vests? she finally asked.

Yes, he said.

Would they be given explosives?

Yes.

How many did they have to make? Because they hardly had reliable enough electricity to make the inventory they were making now, she said.

"They're bringing a generator tomorrow. To 'enjoy improved productivity,' the guy said."

"But fuel costs are—We already have the wiring, or the…that…"

"Transfer switch."

"We would have hooked one up already if we could afford the gas."

"Or the generator."

"Or the generator."

"They're covering it. And they insist on paying for the vests."

"Oh? How nice. And do we charge per vest or per death?"

"I should have asked." He squeezed her hand. "I didn't know what else to do, Bly. With or without us, the vests will be made. And we can use the money. I'd rather not get it this way, but there's no real choice."

And if they demanded more than she and Abe could deliver?

"*We* aren't delivering anything." As far as the guard team knew, he said, Blythe was irrelevant, though the word Abe had chosen was "useless." When challenged by another guard who said he'd been informed the wife did the work—"That's what you said to our man Gregory just last night, wasn't it?"—Abe had pretended that he'd lied. "I told him the guard intimidated me. 'Admitted' I wanted to impress him, but that the fact is I take pride in my merchandise, and if you want something done right," he said as the power and light returned, "you sure as hell don't have a woman do it." He winked at her.

"Oh, for god's sake."

"It worked."

"Of course it worked." She got up and turned off the lamp in the corner. "I should have shot him on the sidewalk instead of hiding in the kitchen like a coward."

Standing to follow her to bed, Abe said he was glad she hadn't, because two more had been waiting at the corner.

Adla watched the clock in her dark bedroom until the red numbers turned to 23:25. She climbed out of bed fully dressed and opened her door slowly, listening for her parents. The house was quiet. She tiptoed barefoot down the hall, past the closed door to her parents' bedroom, past the dark, silent living room, and into the kitchen. She turned the squeaky knob to the door that led to the roof and held her breath, but no one came or yelled at her to get back to bed, so she hurried up the stairs, opened the door, and ran to the edge. She whispered loudly, "Are you there?"

Ruth's head popped up from behind her own wall. "I'm always here. Want a cookie? I already ate mine."

Adla held out cupped hands. Ruth wound up and tossed the cookie underhand over the alley. Adla made a perfect, easy catch and jammed the cookie in her mouth. "Did they come?"

Ruth shook her head.

Both girls crouched at their walls and watched the alley until Adla said her knees were hurting.

"You sit, and I'll watch for them," Ruth said. "Then it's your turn."

Adla sat with her back against the low wall until Ruth whispered that she wanted to sit, now. Adla had just taken over the watch for Ruth when two figures dressed in black and dusted in lamplight appeared at the end of the alley. Both wore caps and had scarves covering their faces. The smaller one leaped from the sandy ground onto a neighbor's shuttered booth, raced cat-like along its narrow counter, and launched into a forward flip, the touchdown almost silent. The larger one raced up a stucco wall, pushed off into a backward flip, and landed with equal grace.

"Ruth!"

Ruth stood and watched, too, as the larger figure vaulted over a trash can at the same time as the smaller one did a side flip, both of them stopping beneath Adla and Ruth. The smaller one looked up at Adla, then used Abe's booth as a platform to reach a higher position and sprang upward, gripping and climbing over Adla's parapet.

Black gloved hands removed scarf and cap, and red hair fell to the young woman's shoulders. She surveyed the rooftop. "This is good for practice," she said. She turned and smiled and said hello to Ruth, who was watching from the other side of the alley.

Ruth, grinning, flapped her hand.

The young woman continued, "We've seen you two so many times, either practicing or looking for us, that he finally said, 'We should just meet them.' That's Alek." She gestured at the person on the ground. "I'm—"

"We know who you are!" Adla squealed, a whisper version.

"You're Emlyn," Ruth said. "Everyone knows about you!"

"You're the best," Adla said. "When I was at school one of the girls I met said her big sister knew you and everyone talked about you."

Ruth pointed into the alley. "And then we saw you right down there one time, and then again and again and we knew it had to be you."

Adla said, "Why do you always come this way?"

Emlyn lifted a shoulder. "We go everywhere. This alley, that alley, rooftops. We go wherever we can."

"Watch me!" Adla jumped onto the parapet before Emlyn could stop her. At the top, she lost her balance and teetered, her weight leaning toward the long fall to the alley.

Emlyn flung her arm out and snatched Adla's t-shirt and yanked her down. "Are you crazy?"

Adla pouted, "I just—"

"Feet together," Emlyn said, pointing at her own feet. "Always feet together. Like this." She demonstrated a jump onto the parapet with Adla and Ruth watching intently. She backflipped onto the rooftop, and Ruth squealed. "Listen," Emlyn said. "Both of you. Never practice on these walls. Not until you're as good as me or Alek. Do you hear me?"

Adla said, a bit too loud, "But you're so old. It'll take forever."

"Old!" she said. Light laughter sounded from below. With a finger held to her lips, Emlyn smiled. "We're only eighteen. And it won't take you that long. It didn't take us that long. But you can't think about how long it's taking or how long it might take. You just have to get better until you're better, and you can't be on the wall until then. All right?"

Both girls nodded.

"If you promise me that, I promise to come back to teach you as often as I can. But if I see you on the wall even one time—"

"We promise," Adla and Ruth whispered together. "We promise!"

Ruth raised her hand for Emlyn's attention. "Can you teach us something now before you go? But we already know about jumping, so something else."

Emlyn beckoned to the girls, drawing them as close together as they all could get on their respective rooftops. She spoke just loud enough for Ruth to also be able to hear. "What I'm going to say will sound boring, but it's important, so listen. Parkour is more than fun climbing and jumping. Your body is moving in new ways, almost like a cat instead of like a person. You have to be strong so you don't hurt yourself."

Adla groaned. "Exercise."

"Alek will tell you what happened to him. He didn't like exercise, either." She poked her head over the parapet and whispered, "Alek." When there was no response, she cupped her hands around her mouth and made a faint noise that sounded like a monkey screaming.

Alek stepped out of the shadows. "Was that supposed to be a grackle?" he whispered.

Emlyn flipped him the finger, then beckoned him to join her on the roof.

Alek told Adla and Ruth the story of falling from a high ledge he hadn't yet had the strength to hold onto. After the young girls made appropriate noises of pain over his injuries, Emlyn went to the center of Adla's rooftop so her movements would also be visible to Ruth. "Practice this to start building arm and core—that's your middle—strength," she said. With her butt and heels touching the ground, her back straight, her knees bent, and her palms flat on the rooftop, she lifted herself until her elbows were straight and swung forward with her heels steadying her, then sat. She repeated the movement swinging backward. "Your feet will come up later," she said. "Adla, you try it."

Adla tried it. "I can't do it."

Emlyn patted her upper arms. "Here." She patted her stomach. "And here. Less feet. Try again. Ruth, you too."

Adla tried again and was doing better until her arms gave out and she dropped hard on her butt. "Ow!"

Ruth giggled.

"You do it, then!"

Ruth mimicked the move.

"Nice," Alek said.

Ruth stuck out her tongue at Adla.

Emlyn showed them two more strength training exercises and had them try. "Make sure you keep your backs str—"

A dull, metal squeak emanated from Ruth's rooftop. She hopped to her feet and looked at the closed door, its handle turning and wiggling. "Reuben," she whispered. She waved Emlyn and Alek away as she backed toward the noise.

Emlyn put on her cap and scarf, tucking away her hair. "We'll be back when we can." She and Alek ran to the edge of the roof. "Train, okay?" She whispered as they climbed over. "Stronger, stronger, stronger."

They were gone.

Ruth dug a key out of her pocket and unlocked the door. Her older brother pushed through in a t-shirt and shorts and took the key from her. He stood over her. "Why was the door locked?" He stuffed the key in his pocket and explored the rooftop, glancing across at Adla and pushing past Ruth to peer over the wall and down into the quiet alley.

The pickup truck parked in front of the Jarvises' house was big and red. Two guards, one younger and of average height and one Abe and Blythe's age, who was unusually tall and uncommonly beautiful, rolled a small black generator to the end of the truck bed and down two wood planks to the ground. Abe led them to the garage for setup, then accompanied them back down the driveway when they were finished.

"This is a good day for you," said the older, tall one, who'd introduced himself in the garage as Citizen Jared Tate, and who seemed to be the one in charge. High, sharp cheekbones that extended into the hidden space under his shaggy, ash-blond hair had the effect of narrowing his eyes into a sinister expression even when he smiled. He nodded a communication at his companion walking back to the truck. "A lot of people would like to have a free generator. I wish I had a free generator."

Abe said, "Can you sew?"

Jared blinked at him. "You're not pleased?"

"Oh, yes. Yes, my family is very excited."

Jared glanced at their front door. "Aren't you going to invite me in?"

"Of course I am." Abe smiled. "Of course. This way."

Blythe and Adla were waiting in the kitchen, Blythe standing in her pink caftan with her loose hair hanging down her back and Adla sitting at the table in shorts and a t-shirt, a book open in front of her. Jared blatantly assessed Blythe, his gaze lingering. She made a flicker of cool eye contact before looking down at her closed-toe sandals.

"Blythe, this is Citizen Tate. My wife Blythe."

"This is Addie." Blythe did not look at Adla. "Say hello to Mr. Tate, Addie."

"If you ever happen to see me at a social function and I'm out of uniform," Jared said pleasantly, "you may call me Mister. But Citizen will do, otherwise." He stepped toward Adla. He held out his hand. "Call me Jared."

Adla put her small hand in his. "Hello."

He squinted his eyes kindly at her. "What are you reading, there?"

Adla leaned forward and ran her finger beneath a line of text. "'There are eleven items every boy should have in a box small enough to fit in his backpack: a needle and thread; a Swiss army knife; a—'"

"How old are you, boy? Eight? Nine?"

Blythe and Abe glanced nervously at each other.

"I'm not—"

Blythe's eyes widened. Adla had already forgotten.

"The child is seven," Abe said quickly.

"Shouldn't you be further along?" Jared spun the book and fanned the pages, stopping just past the middle. "Your class should be well into navigation by now."

"This isn't a first reading, of course," Abe said.

"A second reading? You don't say. That's very impressive, young man." He smiled at Adla. "A destined leader of men. Tell me, Addie—like the baseball player, I assume?" He raised his eyebrows at Abe, who nodded. "Tell me, why does a compass—"

A crashing sound and a yelp had them all turning to look out the window, where the other guard was bent over, clutching one of his hands in the other. Jared hurried out the kitchen door to help with the fuel tank.

"I didn't anticipate that," Blythe said. "I thought it would be a hello and goodbye."

"We shouldn't have let him see her. I told you it was a bad idea."

Blythe started to argue again the same point she had made that morning—that they would see Abe's having a son as also having something to lose, making him fearful in their eyes, more trustworthy—but Jared interrupted by calling to Abe for help with the fuel tank. Abe kissed Adla on the head and ran out.

Blythe looked outside, where all three men were struggling, now. To Adla she said, "Wherever it is you go when I can't find you, go there now in case that man comes back."

Emlyn stepped away from watching Adla and Ruth's sliding exercise to check the alley. Alek's hand emerged from a shadow, gave a thumbs-up, and pulled back into the darkness. She returned her attention to the girls.

"Very good," she said. "Now, watch me." She stood with her black sneakers slightly spread apart and her arms out straight in front of her parallel to the ground. She lowered into a deep squat, then rose, her arms held steady throughout.

"That's easy!" Adla spread her bare feet, stuck out her arms, dropped into a squat, and fell backward.

Ruth laughed at her, then tried it herself and toppled onto her side, dirtying her white shorts.

Adla laughed.

A grackle call sounded from below. Emlyn looked over the wall. Alek's head poked into the orange lamp light, everything but his narrowed eyes masked by his scarf. He signaled *OK*, but put a finger to his lips. Emlyn gave him a thumbs-up and went back to Ruth, whose turn it was to have Emlyn on her roof.

"You have to be quieter," she said. "You can laugh, but lock back your voices. Now, try the squat again. As soon as you feel your balance going, stand up. It'll take some time to go all the way down with confidence, but that's okay. Watch me again." She demonstrated. "Notice my feet. Flat the whole time, down and up. Keep your back straight. Fold at the hips." She patted her black leggings at the hips. "It's called a hip hinge, because you—Never mind. It doesn't matter. Just learn it. Try again."

~

Blythe returned from the bathroom and climbed back into bed, resting her head on Abe's chest. The oil lamp on the dresser flickered.

"Pretty risqué of you to go out there like that." He stroked her bare back. "What would our daughter think?"

Blythe settled into him, wedging her leg between his. "Our daughter," she said with a light tap to his chin, "is otherwise"—*tap*—"occupied."

"Oh?"

"I heard her laughing up there."

"Why didn't you get her?"

"Because she stopped."

"Good. I hate it when she's happy."

Blythe giggled. "Well, she didn't make any more noise, so I let her be."

"You told her not to play up there."

"I know." Blythe looked at the closed curtains, secured with a clip. "But I hated doing it even if it was the logical thing. 'Logical.' Imagine logic in a time like this." She propped herself on an elbow and looked down at him. "What does logic mean to a little girl, our little girl, who sagged her way to bed after we reminded her to stay in? How can we keep her prisoner, Abe? It makes us every bit as cruel as they are." She traced a finger along his collarbone. "Life is so short."

"Shorter if she's careless."

Blythe flopped onto her back. "It could be shorter even if she's careful. She only has to do one little thing wrong, and…"

"The longer she doesn't do one little thing wrong, the longer she'll have."

"But it's no kind of life." She again lifted herself on an elbow. "It's our fault, I know. We were awful to bring her into this. But we did it, and it's done. Now we have to fix it. How can we not allow her to live?"

"We didn't know it would be like this."

"It was already bad enough, and you know it."

Abe eased her back down and ran his fingers through her hair.

Blythe pulled up the sheet and tucked it around them. "I like to think of her on the roof," she murmured. "She must feel the way I felt before the confinement." She yawned. "I wish I'd known it was coming."

"What would you have done?"

The lamp's fire dulled to a short, deep orange flame, then extinguished without Blythe replying.

Abe said, "That many things, eh?"

She laughed. "Isn't it funny? I can't think of a single one. I guess I would do everything I already did, but more. Maybe I would have sat longer in the café. But a person can only drink so much coffee." After a few minutes, she said, "Abe?"

"Mm?"

"I want to take her into town soon."

"Sure. When?" He didn't know how long he should be away from the booth during the week, he said. He apologized. His schedule used to be flexible. Now there was no telling when or whether guards would come by, and if they couldn't find him at the booth they would expect him to be inside making their vests. They might knock. If he didn't answer, they might assume he wasn't taking his responsibility to men and country seriously. "Next weekend," he said.

"No," Blythe said. "I mean, just me. And her."

He rubbed his eyes. "We talked about this."

"But we didn't come to a—"

"Making her look like a boy might not be the better option. I told you. What happens when she gets older and—you know?"

Then she would simply have to tape them down, Blythe said, or do whatever else was necessary to be convincing. But as a girl, Blythe argued (adding that it was a more likely scenario than her being caught in the wrong clothes), Adla could be here one day and the forcibly impregnated wife of one of those monsters the next. "One who would probably beat her, and…and invite all of his monster friends to—"

"Stop." He tugged her hair gently. "Don't make me imagine."

Blythe laid an arm over his chest. It would make the most sense, she said, to start taking Adla out regularly as soon as possible since she had just played a boy in front of a stranger and the experience was fresh.

"I like tomorrow, then," he said. "I don't want you home when they deliver the explosives."

Late the next morning, Adla was safe in her hiding place. Blythe and Abe were in the living room, Abe reading and rereading paragraphs in the newspaper spread out on the coffee table while Blythe braided, separated, and re-braided a section of her hair.

"They're late," she said.

"You don't have to wait. I said I didn't want you here in the first place."

"And, yet, here I—"

The alley-access door rattled under hard pounding. Abe jumped up and opened it to an armed, skinny man in his early twenties with dull blue eyes and pale skin. The oversized duffel bag hanging from his shoulder dragged half of his body down. He wedged his fingers under the strap and struggled to transfer the bag to Abe without dropping it.

"Explosives, wires, detonators. Diagram's in the bag. Jared wants the first ten in five days." He stroked the rifle at his chest, spun on a heel, and strutted down the alley.

Abe closed the door.

THREE YEARS LATER

Adla and Ruth lowered into squat stretches in the centermost points of their respective rooftops. Winter meant early darkness, but the booths below were still open to customers and it was hours until curfew. Neither wanted to risk their movements being captured under the light of the street lamps. When it was loud with voices they could at least get away with whispering across the alley, but it had been only murmured conversations between booth owners and potential customers for the last hour, so they stayed quiet.

Ruth nodded for time and they changed position, stretching one leg straight out to the side while keeping the other bent, heel flat to the ground. Each picked up a brick, kept close by for exercises like these, and held it in one hand for a count of five, then shifted balance to bend the straight leg and straighten the bent leg, all while holding their bricks steady. Their faces pinched with the effort.

"And just like that, not a mark in sight," one of the booth men shouted. "Break time!" The others commiserated loudly over the crinkling sound of plastic chip bags tearing open and soda cans popping.

Ruth ran a little closer to the edge of her roof and, re-tying her long ponytail, whispered across to Adla that she wanted to do safety rolls, next.

"Me, too. Look!" Adla stepped closer and lifted the back of her sweatshirt, exposing bruises on one side.

Ruth raised her own sweatshirt and showed her bruises.

"Yours are as bad as mine."

"I know!" Ruth rubbed her back. "I don't know why these stupid rolls are so hard to do."

"I wish Emlyn would just let us practice with blankets."

"You can if you want to. She won't do anything."

"I know."

They returned to their squat stretches.

Ruth whispered loudly, "I saw the Parker Brothers' new music video last night."

Adla stopped mid-stretch. "Lucky!"

"I know. Reuben fell asleep and I had the internet to myself. Ever since your parents gave us a generator he's almost always on. I never get to use it."

"I thought he won't let you watch music videos."

"That's why I did it when he was sleeping. I go to the boring sites he says I can go to when he's around just because it's at least something else to do."

"I'd rather be on the roof all day long than be on a computer."

"Except in summer!" Ruth began, "'Its fall display will cross your eyes'…"

"'The winter sunsets mesmerize'…"

"'Spring's wildflowers can beat the sky'…"

Adla grinned. "'But the summer dust is really shit'…"

"'And the heat will make you want to die'!"

They snorted and snickered with their hands over their mouths.

Blythe, smiling at the girls' remembered, somehow, schoolyard poem, crept down from the rooftop stairs and made salads to go with the stew in the crockpot. When she finished, she noticed she'd left the light on in the sewing room, its door open a crack. She went down the hall and into the room and studied it, taking an inventory of everything visible to confirm there were no traces of their vest work. Satisfied, she turned off the light, went to her spot on the living room couch, opened her laptop, and navigated as she did every evening to the *West Coast Daily News* website.

TWENTY KILLED IN NEWBYRL, NEVADA SUICIDE BOMBING was the front-page headline.

In three years, such an attack had happened locally only one other time, when, the year before, a man previously known in hushed circles to oppose the Institution had announced his candidacy for Board of Education Chairman. Blythe and Abe had watched the coverage of the aftermath of Cosmo Pitkin's death—and of those who'd had the bad luck to be in close proximity to him—all night. Their wine-fueled discussion had moved from "They could have just taken him to the clearing" to "Why not let him run for office? He wouldn't have won even with the votes" to the realization that the government had wanted more than to simply make him go away. In the short period between Pitkins's announcement and his death, he'd invigorated a small but disruptive faction that, without the right kind of discouragement, would have grown. Since the bombing at the bookstore where Cosmo Pitkin and ten other dead innocent adults had been shopping, no one had dared to publicly oppose the local government.

There had, of course, been similar attacks throughout the country over the years, but Blythe and Abe had been able to assume their distance from the locations made their involvement unlikely. They chose to ignore the fact that they had delivered a consistent supply of inventory for three years that, if not detonated in Newbyrl, must have been going somewhere to be used for something.

It was harder to pretend they'd had nothing to do with the Newbyrl deaths. While they had no proof that they'd made the vest the attacker had used on Cosmo Pitkin—others had also naturally been recruited to supply vests, both in the state and across the country—they were almost certain they were the only ones making them in Newbyrl.

Blythe kept reading: *Sixteen adults and four children were killed when a suicide bomber detonated explosives at a restaurant believed to be a secret meeting location frequented by subversives. …*

Luigi's Italian Restaurant manager Kelly Lake claimed to have no knowledge of the use of the restaurant's basement wine cellar by the underground opposition group believed to have been the bomber's target. "So sad little children had to die," Lake said. He added, "Their parents should've known better."

…Mayor's official response was to condemn "the senseless slaughter of innocent civilians." He had no further comment.

Blythe slammed the laptop closed. She opened it, then slammed it closed again and stood up and threw it to the floor. She lifted a corner of the couch and slid the laptop under its wide, wood foot and dropped the couch, lifted it, and dropped it again.

The door opened from the alley and Abe stuck his head in, cheeks pink and eyes bright from the chill. "I have to—What's going on?"

She told Abe, who listened from the open doorway, what she had read about the attack on the restaurant, including the details of the casualties.

He looked at her for a long time with his mouth open as if he had something to say, but saying nothing.

"I know. You have to go. Right?" Blythe marched across the room. She took his face in her hands and kissed his forehead, his cheek, his lips.

He said, "I'll try to be back for dinner."

"Don't try." She gently pushed him into the alley. "Those men are very fragile, and they have to believe they're the priority."

Blythe watched Abe through a narrow sliver of open door until he disappeared around the corner with another booth owner, then went to the kitchen and added croutons to the salads and got out the dressings she and Adla liked. She called her daughter to dinner, but Adla didn't come. She brushed her hands on her pants and headed upstairs, going only far enough to see Adla's head through the space made by a rock propping the door open.

She watched as Adla practiced decent, but still imperfect, rolls, and took another step up. Left behind on the top stair was the book Adla had been carrying when she'd told Blythe she wanted to go outside to "read."

Adla whispered loudly to Ruth, "I think I got it!"

"Not me." Ruth rubbed her lower back. "I keep hitting my bone. What do you do?"

"I just—"

Blythe scraped the stairs to make it sound like she was coming up and cupped her hands around her mouth for the illusion of distance. "Aaadlaaa!"

Adla hushed Ruth with her finger and ignored her mother. She and Ruth started doing cartwheels.

Blythe noiselessly eased the door open, going unnoticed by both girls until Ruth landed upright and spotted her standing in the doorway behind Adla.

Adla whispered, "Yours is better than min—"

"Hi, Mrs. Jarvis," Ruth said quietly.

Adla spun around.

"Hello, Ruth. How are you?" Blythe stepped out. "How are your parents and brother?"

"They're—we're—all very thankful for the generator, Mrs. Jarvis"

"Oh, please don't." She waved the words away. "I only wish we could buy them for the whole neighborhood."

Ruth said her parents had been sharing theirs with two of their neighbors who had brought over so many cupcakes and bread loaves to thank them that her mother had had to start throwing them away. "Reuben wouldn't let anyone eat them, anyway, because he said they were bad for us." She used her hands to mime a big belly and puffed out her cheeks. "But at least my dad's home more now that he can work from the computer and doesn't have to travel all the time."

"You must enjoy that," Blythe whispered. She tucked her hands inside the cuffs of her sweater sleeves and wrapped her arms around herself. "Adla, time to come in.—Don't forget your book." She said goodbye to Ruth and started toward the door with Adla trailing behind her.

"See you tomorrow," Ruth said.

Blythe stopped, making Adla bump into her back. She turned. "Tomorrow? Oh, no, are you not feeling well, Ruth?"

Adla and Ruth looked at Blythe, confused.

"Or are you going somewhere with your family? Will you be gone later tonight?"

The girls looked at each other.

"Well, I know Adla isn't sick. Are you, walnut?"

"No, Mama."

"In that case, I don't know why you wouldn't see each other at the regular time tonight. Eleven-thirty, isn't it?"

Adla looked up at her mother open-mouthed.

Ruth smiled. "Yes, Mrs.——"

Reuben flung open the door behind Ruth, knocking over a basket of clothes stationed in front of it. "I'm sick of coming up here to get you." He looked down at the basket and kicked at some folded shirts that had fallen out. "How long does it take to get the laundry? Mom said——" He noticed Blythe.

An automatic smile of greeting started on Blythe's lips. It dissolved at Reuben's disapproving glare, which began at her breasts—their shape somewhat visible under her fitted sweater—and traveled down the length of her tight jeans.

Blythe crossed her arms over her chest, said, "Adla," and hurried to the door and into the stairwell, stubbing her toe on the rock and banging her shoulder on the door frame. From the stairwell she called her daughter again. "Inside. Now."

Adla followed her in, kicking the rock out of the way.

"I'm telling Dad to keep the roof off limits from now on unless I'm with you so you don't get distracted," Reuben's voice boomed through the closed door. "Pick up the clothes!"

"…difficult losses, including the occasional child casualty. It's hard. Granted. Tragic. But in the scheme of things, it's an acceptable loss." Behind the speaker, a theater-sized screen displayed his head and shoulders, the writing on his black baseball cap—ORDER IN RANKS—blinding white. Because of the size of the screen, there was no way for Abe, or anyone else at Replenishment who might not want to give the man their attention, to avoid looking at him without turning fully away. The guards would surely notice. "An acceptable loss, yes. Because the ultimate goal is safeguarding the hierarchy. Look, we are defending—When you get right down to it, we are defending every person's constitutional right to exist in a peaceful and functioning society. One that isn't mired in confusion and infighting and power struggles. Those things lead to a lack of civility. Low productivity. They cause expensive—in terms of both money and human life, now— cracks in the foundation of this great nation. But that's what these irritant groups want. And did you hear? There's a new one, now. Oh, yeah. Even after Luigi's. And what they want is, they want to go back. Back to that confusion, that infighting, that death of progress and industry.

"Now, I can't explain why anyone would want that, but— well, if I could explain it, that would mean I understood it, and if I understood it, I'd have to shoot myself. I would. I would shoot myself in the head. Because I don't want to understand it. I don't want to understand why someone—why those traitors scurrying around Luigi's dank basement like rats—would want to go back to a time before the hierarchy. Back when some ill-conceived and fraudulent notion of 'equality' actually convinced people to take it up as a cause until it ate away at society like a cancer. I don't want to understand those hairy, screeching whales of the past who succeeded—and they succeeded for a time, they did—in disempowering men. Neutering us. Even equating our basic manhood with toxicity.

"*Toxicity*. Do you know what toxic means? Poisonous. Do you know what it's like to have someone look at you—to not even know you, but to look at you and see poison? 'Equality.' That's what they said they wanted, the word they used. Genius. 'Equality.' Forget the hierarchy! That's what they said. Who needs it, they said. But here's what happened. That 'equality' initiative that endeavored to establish men and women as peers led to nothing but chaos. That's right. No one knew who was supposed to be doing what. Men and women were like ants forced off their trusted scent trail. It was a holy mess. The only hierarchy operating at that time existed in the order of destruction: first it was families, then societies. If they'd been allowed to go on even a little bit longer they would have decimated an entire civilization.

"Let that sink in. Ponder on it. Really ponder on it any time you feel bad about the harmless young innocents those traitorous rats got killed at Luigi's. We are defending something bigger than what can be measured in the loss of a single young life. Or even in the loss of four young lives. Look at how vast a civilization is. See the big picture. Do you see it? I know you do. So you also know, then, that we do what we must do. And one thing, the first and most important thing, we must do is stand together. When men stand together, greatness is achieved. But we cannot do it alone. And we cannot fight among ourselves. We cannot fracture. Our job is too big. We are, and must continue to be, a tribe of men united. United in our love of country, and united in our commitment to preserve order. Thank you."

Roaring and clapping broke out for the bearded man on the stage that spanned the width of the massive room. Abe whistled and clapped and pumped his fist in the air to fit in, watching the others and waiting for one of them to be the first to head toward the exit so he could follow. On stage, the speaker removed his sport coat and draped it over the shoulder of his polo, then bowed. Abe looked around again. A cluster of five guards, Jared among them, was standing at the bottom of the stairs leading up to the stage. Abe had been to enough of these to know they would circle the motivational speaker when he came down and pat his back all the way out the door. For now, they were simply waiting, nodding now and then at something one of the others had said, disinterested in the deafening enthusiasm surrounding them.

Abe was about to scan the crowd again when Jared noticed him. He raised his chin at Abe. Abe raised his chin back. Jared commanded him over with a subtle jerk of his head. Abe pushed through the horde.

~

Adla adjusted herself on her bed, kicking off her books and notes, and blew at the clear polish on her fingernails. She hadn't known when she'd sneaked it from her mother's bathroom that it would take so long. She'd also messed it up even after Ruth, whose fingernails had always been shiny, lately, had warned, "You'll get it on your finger, and then you'll wipe it off, but you'll also wipe some of it off your nail, and then you'll put more on but it'll be uneven. My mom says you have to 'be slow and precise.'" Adla had tried but had gotten impatient. She blew at the nails again, then touched one of the shiny surfaces with her fingertip. Dry. She rolled off the mattress, gripped the underside of the box spring, and slid the bed away from the wall.

In the kitchen, Blythe finished mashing bananas in a bowl and dumped the last of the flour into a measuring cup. She came up short by at least a quarter cup. She went into her bedroom and threw her pink caftan on over her clothes. "Adla!"

Adla landed on her comforter after a successful vault over the foot of the bed, whose frame stood at least six inches higher than the mattress. She bounced off, ran to the end, and positioned herself for another.

Blythe, a pink pashmina wrapped around her arms and shoulders, swished down the hall and opened Adla's door, startling her mid-vault.

Adla jerked her leg and flubbed her landing. She grumbled.

"I need flour," Blythe said.

"I don't have it."

"I know you don't have—We have to go the store."

"What about dinner and Daddy?"

"I don't know when he's coming home, but we won't be gone very long." Blythe ran her fingers through Adla's hair in the opposite direction of its natural growth until it looked messy, rough. "We only have forty-five minutes until curfew. Please put your shoes on. And a jacket."

"Is he still at Replenishment?"

"Yes, Adla." She saw Adla's books—*Woman: Strong and Silent* and *The Fellowship of Men*—on the floor. "Now, shoes and jacket or I'll quiz you on *Strong and Silent*."

"Could I get quizzed on *Fellowship of Men*?"

"Shoes and jacket."

Before opening the door to the alley, Blythe looked down at her daughter, who easily passed for a son. "Rules?"

"Don't talk to anyone unless I have to, don't…uh…don't say a lot, and…um…"

"No di—"

"No distractions!"

"Good."

Blythe, holding Adla's hand, guided her down the main street's sidewalk, weaving through mostly boys and men. When they did pass another girl or woman, and they did this only a few times, she was also in a pink or, if older, gray caftan and accompanied by a man who more often than not was carrying either an AR-15 or a Desert Eagle (Abe had both) and could have been any of the other men: the same high hairstyle, the same sport coat and polo, the same basic slacks with the same sharp center creases. They weren't even ordered to do it, which Blythe had told Abe was something she found amusing.

"Mama." Adla whispered, tugging Blythe's hand. "I think I know that girl."

Blythe looked where Adla discreetly pointed. A girl Adla's age, her long hair professionally curled and tapping the shoulders of what, at her age, should have been a white caftan, was walking with a man who appeared to be in his late forties, if not early fifties. Her right hand was in his left.

"From school?" Blythe said.

"I think so but maybe not."

"You were only there a month, walnut. You can't expect to remember." Blythe tried not to stare at the little girl's wan face and tormented eyes as they got closer. She instinctively checked her left hand. A gold ring circled the young girl's ring finger.

"Mind your business," the man growled under his breath as they passed.

"Nope," Adla said. "It wasn't her I don't think. I don't know." She shrugged, and they walked on.

A group of boys Adla's age wearing their chosen uniform of some variation of a thin corduroy jacket, t-shirt, and jeans were socializing outside the grocery store as Blythe and Adla approached. One of them noticed Adla and didn't look away.

Adla, operating on something her mother had once told her about how dangerous it could be to look afraid, calmly turned and pointed at something in the opposite direction and said, "Look at that."

Blythe looked, saw nothing, then spotted the boys clustered on the sidewalk. "Oh, yes, I see it now." She chattered on, keeping her daughter's head turned away from the boys until they were safely inside the store.

The baking aisle was neatly stocked with a single brand of each product, each in only one size. Blythe pulled the five-pound bag of flour off the shelf, told Adla to make a basket, and rested the flour in the bowl of Adla's arms and chest. "Got it?"

"Easy!"

"You're getting strong."

She followed Adla to the front and waited as she heaved the bag onto the counter. The gray-haired, red-cheeked man behind the register smiled down. "Anything else?"

Adla shook her head.

"Twenty-four seventy-eight."

Adla looked at Blythe, who started to hand her a credit card.

"Sorry, little man. Cash only," he said. "Internet problems."

Blythe pulled a few folded bills from her pocket and gave Adla a twenty and a ten, which Adla slapped onto the counter, her shiny nails on display. Blythe grasped her hand and pushed it down to her side. "That was too much." She pretended to search her wallet. "I thought I had something smaller."

"About time you start carrying some cash of your own, isn't it, boy?" The cashier tapped in the total. The drawer shot open with a ding. "Independence." He counted the change, then pulled out one dollar at a time from under the spring-loaded arm. "A man needs independence!" He slid the bills and coins across the counter at Adla. "You keep that."

Adla hesitated, and Blythe gently kicked her ankle. Adla stuffed the money in her pocket.

Blythe and Adla took a right outside of the store and went the long way to avoid the boys on the sidewalk, who had moved across the street and would be encountered again if they went home the way they'd come. It was a nicer walk than their normal route. There were more paved roads and sidewalks, fewer packed-sand alleys that coated the hem of Blythe's caftan with beige dust. This way brought them down a relatively new and picturesque pedestrian street with no sidewalks and an assortment of shops, bars, restaurants, and barbers. Cape myrtles under perpetual spotlights, their peeling trunks and branches glowing brown and green, created a visual barrier between the walking area and, built in the lot where a failed hotel had been torn down, an expansive sport park. The lodge—a big, square building with tall windows, massive wood doors, and a ten-foot-high cast iron longhorn sculpture out front—was just two blocks behind it. Blythe looked around for Abe in case he was on his way home, but he was nowhere on the street.

Adla slipped from Blythe's grip to stop and watch a small group of teenage boys practicing flips, jumps, sweeps, and vaults over the park's benches, rails, and walls. One boy was focused on reverse vaults. Another ran up to a tree, jumped, planted a foot on the trunk, and propelled himself from there to the top of a short wall. He ran down it, flipped, hit the ground and rolled, then jumped up again and ran off to another—

Adla's hand was suddenly in Blythe's again and she was being dragged away.

Blythe filled two bowls with stew and asked Adla to bring them to the table. "One at a time. They're hot." She turned to get another bowl from the cabinet and stopped at a dull crashing sound.

"I thought I could do it."

One of the bowls had made it to the table. The other was a mosaic of porcelain pieces mixed with splattered stew on the floor. Adla's head was down, her eyes looking up but not quite meeting Blythe's.

"Like I said." Blythe put a hand on her hip. "Hot."

"Yeah."

"How are your fingers?" She walked around the mess and looked at Adla's hand. "Do they hurt?"

Adla shook her head.

Blythe kissed her small fingertips, then peeled some paper towels from the roll, slid the trash can over, and set the rest of the roll on the table. "Don't worry," she said, plucking out all the pieces of broken dish. "We have more than enough. Clean the rest of this up, and we'll eat."

Adla had just made the first wet sweep with a wad of paper towels when Abe barged into the kitchen. He dropped a duffel bag on the floor and slammed the door behind him. To Adla he said, "Go to the roof."

"But I have to—"

"Now, please."

"Go ahead." Blythe tipped the trash can for Adla's used paper towels.

Adla dropped them in and ran out toward her bedroom.

"Drink before dinner?" Abe said, looking at the stew still on the floor.

"Of course. What happened?"

Adla zipped past the kitchen with her sneakers dangling from her fingers. The door to the roof banged against the wall, then thudded shut.

Abe poured one for each of them, then took the glasses in one hand and the duffel bag in the other to their sewing room while Blythe finished with the paper towels and a wet rag. By the time she was able to join him, he'd arranged a pile of plastic explosive blocks in front of him on the carpet, where he was sitting with what was left of his drink propped on his knee.

"They're too small." Blythe grabbed her glass from the sewing table and joined him on the floor.

"Oh, no. They're exactly the right size." He downed the rest of his whisky, got up, and left the room. When he came back, he was carrying the bottle. He plopped on the floor, filled his glass, and added to Blythe's.

She picked up one of the small explosives and turned it over in her hand. "The vest that would fit these would have to be small enough for someone Adla's age."

"Mm."

"Even younger."

"Could be." He sipped his drink.

"Who is this for?—I know they don't tell you, but have you heard anything?"

The most he had heard, he said, were complaints of another local "irritant group." Or it was possible that the group that had been targeted at Luigi's had another branch. Either way, the team had apparently decided that the best way to gain access to them while also delivering a powerful message was to make use of a child.

"No one would stand for the government doing something like that." Blythe scraped her fingernail along the rim of her glass. "Really. Children? Not even people who believe—"

"Ah, but but but. You forget. As far the public knows, it's faction on faction violence. It has nothing to do with the government."

"So we'll tell them."

Abe shrugged. "People have tried to assign responsibility to them before. No one believes it." And to be extra sure no one believed it, Abe said, the government always denied the charges, suggested the accusers were mentally unstable or desperate for attention, and allowed them to go on living. "We'll delay," he said. "It's something, at least. I'll forget a wire. They'll probably assume it's sabotage. They'll be right, of course, but I can—I'll call it an error. It's the best we can do."

"What will they do if they don't believe you?"

"One of two things. Both will kill me."

"We can leave," she said quietly. "We can run."

"There's nowhere to run, Bly."

"But if we don't run, they'll kill you."

"And if we do run, they'll find and kill all of us."

"You can go alone."

"Like I said, they'll find and kill—Even if I did make it to some magical place of safety, you don't think they'd break down our door and get you and Adla if I disappeared?" He took a slow drink, looked into his glass. He raised his eyes to Blythe. "Take her," he said. "Leave in the morning."

"Absolutely not."

Emlyn supervised Adla's and Ruth's kong hop practice from Ruth's rooftop. Ruth was more graceful in her movements, her legs smoothly tucking toward her outstretched, planted hands with each hop. Adla kept up, pace-wise, but her hops were jerky, and her feet hit the roof hard.

"Are we the only girls that do this?" Adla panted.

"Oh, no."

Ruth stood and wiped her forehead with her sweatshirt. "How many are there?"

"Ten, maybe fifteen?"

"Are they older?" Ruth asked.

"Are they better than us?" Adla added.

"They're about your age." Emlyn pulled at one of her gloves to tighten it on her hand. "Some a little older, some a little younger. Some better, some not."

"How come they're all our age?" Ruth said.

"Because most of the girls my age were scared off. Some of the other ones wanted to keep practicing, but they didn't like doing it inside and they were too scared to be on their roofs at night, so they quit." She tucked her hair into her cap and put on her scarf.

Adla said, "Why didn't that happen to you?"

Emlyn smiled. "I love it too much." She swung herself over the parapet and disappeared.

Adla ran to the edge of the roof and looked down. Alek was coming out of the shadows to join Emlyn. "Where are you going now?" Adla whisper-shouted.

As she and Alek made their way down the alley, Emlyn spread her arms wide over her head as if to say, *Anywhere.*

Adla looked at Ruth. "Let's follow them!"

"Ha," Ruth said, then saw the not-kidding expression on Adla's face. "Really?"

"Don't you want to?"

"I don't think we…It's not safe, and…" Ruth whispered, "Yes!"

They met in the alley after hurrying into dark clothes and sneaking out their side doors, neither quite practiced enough to fall from rooftops. Adla's costume was easier, thanks to her short hair. Ruth had had to gather all of hers under her dad's knit cap, but worn along with the jacket and pants, she was still a convincing enough boy.

They ran down their alley to the side street, looking up and down for Emlyn and Alek. They continued on when they didn't spot them, putting practical use to what Emlyn called "quadrupedal" exercises in order to stay in the lower shadows cast by cars and trash bins. Their hands were so used to the hard, rough texture of their rooftops that running and hopping on all fours didn't present them with a new challenge, even if the distance did.

They started to get tired, and Adla was about to suggest they go home when she remembered the sport park and said they should check there. Adla and Ruth stayed off the main road, taking alleys and side streets past dark abandoned houses and coming up on the park from behind the steak house. The obstacles were deserted, the leftover light from the crape myrtles' lamps just bright enough to reveal the steep and shallow ramps, high and low rails, short and long low walls, and various sizes of cement blocks.

"And they have these trees and all these buildings to practice on, too." Adla sighed. "I could spend a whole month—"

A high-pitched whistle echoed down the street.

Adla and Ruth scrambled backward into the alley and along the steakhouse's wall until they were fully in the shadow.

The whistle again. A deep voice yelled from afar, "Skeet!"

"What!" The second one was nearby. On the street, somewhere.

"Where you at?"

"Headin' back to switch with Lonnie." His voice was closer, now.

"I said where you at, not what're you doing. I know what time it is. Where you at?"

"By the gym," he said, and Adla and Ruth crouched and curled themselves into tight balls under the dark cover. "Where you at?"

"Joe's Barber. Hurry up."

A tall guard, a rifle dangling at his side and a pistol in a holster on his hip, appeared across the street and took his time walking past the sport park in long, smooth strides, his arms swaying grandly. "Y'know," he shouted, "if they'd let us stay in those rooms in the lodge instead of sticking us in the shack, we'd almost be home." He stopped to scan the park, crouching and shifting from one side to the other to see past the trees. Satisfied, he straightened, stretched his back, and moved languidly on.

"I don't know," the other one yelled. "If they let us use those fancy rooms in the lodge the girls might get the idea we want 'em for somethin' more."

"Oh, hell naw. No whores in the lodge. Keep the shack for the snacks." Skeet laughed.

The other man guffawed.

Skeet glanced briefly toward Adla and Ruth's alley, took another step, then sighed, stopped, and turned to face them directly. He stared unmoving into the dark.

"What do we do?" Ruth's whisper was so low it was almost inaudible.

"What would Emlyn do?"

Ruth shrugged. "Run?"

Skeet closed his eyes tight, squinting hard, then opened them into narrow lines and looked again, his head craned slightly forward.

"We'll run if he comes over," Adla whispered. "He'll think we're boys at least, anyway, breaking curfew or something."

"But what if he catches—"

"Hey, uh, if anyone's in the alley," Skeet said, "it'd be a lot easier on me if you'd just come out." He rolled his neck, stretching, then laughed to himself. "About face!" He spun dramatically on the sidewalk, clicked his heels, saluted the trees, and marched down the street. His slow footfalls echoed, then faded.

Ruth stood and adjusted her hair in her cap. "Let's go home. We're never going to find them."

"There!" Adla whispered, pointing over Ruth's shoulder. Two dark-clad figures were racing across an intersection at the opposite end of the alley.

The girls ran after them.

It wasn't difficult to track Emlyn and Alek through the small town center's streets and alleys. Their acrobatics slowed them down. When they went directly up, Adla and Ruth could pause, catch their breath, and be ready to run again when the two inevitably touched down—which they frequently did. Many of the rooftops were too far apart for even them to jump from one to the next, and those connected in a strip posed no challenge, so they didn't spend much time on them once they worked their way up.

Adla and Ruth followed Emlyn and Alek around the block, back down the pedestrian street, and through the sport park, where they caught the end of one of Alek's backflip dismounts from the highest rail. They were seconds behind, about to follow them across a small, dark intersection at the edge of town, when Ruth stopped short and grabbed Adla's sleeve and said, "Look."

The brass plaque bolted to the wall a foot above their heads shined as if new. *May we be forever undeterred in our resolve to protect the weak, the innocent, and the defenseless from the indignities, wrongs, and outrages of the lawless named below.* "Reuben told me about this." Ruth reached up and ran her finger along two of the engraved names stacked one on top of the other: *Oliver*

Jarvis. Katherine Jarvis. "He said your family was here, but I didn't believe him." She stepped back to allow space for Adla.

Adla touched the names, too. "They died in the fighting when the government came. My dad told me."

"My brother said the government killed them because they were traitors."

Adla smiled. "I think we're traitors."

Ruth smiled back.

They ran across the intersection and into the dark, stumbling over the rocky terrain and snagging their pants and scratching their shins and ankles on tough desert shrubs. Their eyes were adjusted to the light of the moon and stars, and their footing surer, when they reached the near edge of the clearing. In the distance, the silhouettes of Emlyn and Alek shrank toward the olive trees.

"Don't walk there!" Ruth grabbed Adla's arm to stop her near a mound of rocks and sand. "Reuben told me about this place." She led her around dark patches that stood out like inkblots against the cool blue ground.

Adla looked over her shoulder at them as they kept walking. "What is that stuff?"

"Blood."

Emlyn was reclining against Alek, his back supported by a tree, when Adla and Ruth were finally near enough to see them and to hear them speaking. Ruth gave the sign for quiet and tapped her ear. They hid behind a tree and listened.

"…taking them too long to get here," Emlyn said. "I think we must have scared them home."

"That was the point."

Adla waved Ruth onward, and the two crept closer, hard earth grating audibly beneath their shoes.

Alek whispered, "They're here."

Ducking and crouching, Adla and Ruth closed in a bit more, falling to their hands and knees to hide behind rocks.

Loud enough for the girls to hear, Emlyn said, "We've done our best, but I just don't think Ruth and Adla are grasping it."

"You're right," Alek played along. "They should be much better than that three years in. Let's give up. It'll free up more time for the ones who take it seriously."

"No!" Adla said.

Ruth shushed her with a "Sh!"

Emlyn and Alek laughed, and Adla and Ruth rushed them, toppling onto Emlyn's lap.

"You were kidding, right?" Adla said.

"Yes, Emlyn, please don't stop teaching us!"

Emlyn tickled them gently. "Alek, can you believe they followed us, the little sneaks? Can you believe it?"

Ruth stole occasional glances at Alek, whose exposed face, which they were seeing for the first time, had made her and Adla exchange a wide-eyed look while they were finding their spots with Emlyn and Alek under the olive tree.

"I was sick the first time I saw the clearing up close." Alek was sitting cross-legged beside a cross-legged Emlyn. He traced a circle on her knee.

"We go around it whenever we come out here," Emlyn said. "Besides, I think it's probably some kind of bad luck to walk too close to it. It's like a grave, in a way."

Adla asked what the people did wrong to get in trouble there.

Emlyn said sharply, "Nothing."

"You followed us because you don't understand." Alek scooped up rocky sand and let it fall between his fingers. "Maybe it hasn't touched you. But it's here. All around you."

"You have to be afraid," Emlyn said.

Adla argued that Emlyn didn't seem afraid.

"I am," she said. "I've been afraid for so long that I almost don't feel it, anymore. But I am."

"They look for her. They've heard of her." Alek bumped Emlyn's shoulder with his. "Everyone has. We walk right by the guards, and they have no idea she's the dainty flower walking next to me."

"But why?" Adla said. "Why are they trying to find you?"

Emlyn rolled her eyes. "Because I have these." She pointed at her chest. "Threatening, right?"

Addressing Adla and Ruth, Alek said, "If you have to be stupid, be smart about it, at least. Don't go out around town at night, even if you really want to."

"And never stop practicing," Emlyn said. "It'll save your life."

"Well…"

"It's better than nothing, Alek."

Blythe added her final stitches to the vest and set it aside. She never touched the plastic or the wiring. Abe would do it when he closed the booth for the day.

Wind blew through the open window and flapped the thin yellow curtain behind the machine. It was a warm day for winter, even in the desert, and the gusts of fresh air were the first after weeks with the windows closed. She slid the vest to her and stroked it absently, running her fingertips along the seams of the small armholes, tracing the narrow shoulders, feeling the excess fabric from the lining pushing up through the waist's cotton shell, ten tiny pockets awaiting their explosives.

Outside, a man laughed.

Blythe's chair tipped back and clattered to the floor with the force of her standing. She reached over the sewing machine, yanked the curtain out of the way, and slammed the window shut.

Abe inspected the wires and their flawed connections to the detonators a sixth time before adding the small vests to the duffel bag. He carried the bag out to the living room and joined Blythe on the couch.

Some silent minutes later came the knocks on the door, and Blythe got out of view while Abe passed the bag to the messenger. He closed the door afterward and didn't turn around. "They pay him a hundred dollars per delivery. Do you think that's why he does it?"

"I don't know." She walked up behind him and put her arms around him, resting her chin on the back of his shoulder. "Abe."

He faced her. They looked at each other for a long time.

Abe knocked on Adla's open bedroom door, making her look up from a workbook she was writing in on her bed. "Busy?"

She tossed the book on the floor. "Ech. No."

"Come with me."

He took her hand and led her to the hallway. Blythe joined them from the living room and the three went up to the roof.

Blythe and Abe sat on the big cement block, and Adla stood nearby and traced lines in the dust with the toe of her sneaker.

"Well?" Blythe said. "Show him."

Adla looked at her father and then at her mother. She shrugged.

"Oh, Adla. Don't treat us like idiots. Just show him."

Adla pulled at her hair. She walked to the far end of the roof, held her hands over her head, and brought them down into a cartwheel, followed by one more. She stood before them, waiting.

"What is this?" Abe said. "I came up here for this? I can do that."

Adla laughed. "Can not!"

Abe raised his eyebrows, stood, walked to the spot where Adla had started her cartwheel, and did one of his own. Adla said, "Wow!"

Sitting back down, he said, "Now. Show me."

"Show him what you can do, walnut, not what you think I think you can do. He just wants to see. I've told him, but my words can't do you justice."

Adla grinned and sprinted across the roof. She got into position, eyeing the space laid out in front of her. After a deep breath, she took a few running steps toward them, sprang into a side flip with her hands gripping her tucked knees, and landed on steady feet.

Her parents cheered quietly and clapped using only their fingertips.

"My god," Abe said, "how much did you have to practice that?"

"Like six hundred times. Watch this!—Oh, you have to get up, though."

Blythe and Abe moved away from the block. Adla ran at it, jumped, dove forward, and planted her palms on the far side, tucking her legs for a vault. Her left foot caught the corner, flipping her onto her side and throwing her to the ground. Blythe and Abe started toward her.

"I'm fine," she said, getting up. She rubbed her arm. "I'm okay. I can do it."

She did it again, this time landing smoothly on the opposite side of the block.

Abe pulled her close and wrapped his arms around her tightly. "Extraordinary."

That night, the three of them ate dinner together in the living room. No one spoke. Adla shoved her last bite in her mouth and asked to be excused.

"What's your hurry?" Abe said. "Sit a minute. Digest. Keep us company."

"But—"

"Adla," Blythe said.

They went back to their silence.

Abe opened his booth in the morning the way he did every morning by wiping down the counter, unlocking and sliding up the shutter, and putting the cash box on its shelf. But this morning he did it while watching both ends of the alley.

Blythe listened to his routine with an ear to the door. It hadn't yet been twenty-four hours since the messenger had come for the duffel bag, but they didn't know how long they would have to wait to learn whether the creative wiring in the vests had been discovered. They didn't know, if it was discovered, whether the guards would blame and immediately punish Abe or simply ask him to fix them. If they did decide he'd betrayed them, she and Abe didn't know whether they would take him from home or wait until a Replenishment.

When it had been quiet outside for some time, Blythe went into the kitchen for another cup of coffee, confident he was still out there. Had someone come to take him, he would have loudly said a phrase they'd made up for him the night before: *Let me just grab my hat*. He didn't wear a hat, but he did own a baseball cap or two. They were keeping one on the kitchen table in case the guard's response was, *Sure. Go ahead.*

Abe was bagging a jacket for a customer near closing time when three guards approached his booth. "Enjoy," he said to the departing customer, his eyes on the guards. They were pointing at items on the shelves behind him, talking among themselves until the customer had gone away.

"So, what do you have, here?" one of the guards said. "Shirts? Jackets?"

Abe was about to answer, but another of the guards had bent to tie his shoelace, and his rifle sling had slipped off his shoulder. The butt of the gun hit the ground, knocking the heavy barrel against his forehead.

The guard's two companions laughed as he stood up.

Abe did not. "Uh…Shirts and jackets. Yes. Caftans. Some vests. Some blankets. What are you looking for?"

The guard with the new bruise on his forehead said, "We're looking for you, Abe."

Blythe was in the middle of making a cake when Abe entered the kitchen from the living room. He cleared his throat, and she spun around with a glass of buttermilk and poppyseeds in her hand.

"Yum," he said. "What's this for?"

"The cake or the dress?"

"Both." He went to her and took the glass and set it on the counter. "I love you in red. And what did you do to your hair?"

"Used a curling iron."

He smiled a small smile. "Why? What is all this?"

"I didn't know what else to do. I couldn't stand at the door listening any time I wasn't sewing. It could go on for months, couldn't it? I'll eventually have to figure out how to live my life without wondering whether this day, this minute, will be the time they come for—"

"This day," he said softly. "This minute." Without releasing her, he reached back and felt around on the kitchen table until he found his baseball cap.

"What happened?" Her eyes were on the hat. "What did they say?"

"They said they want me to go with them."

"But they didn't say where? Or why?"

"That was all they said." He put the cap on. "Tell Adla—"

"I'm not telling her anything. It's nothing. This is nothing. It's not the first time they've made you go with them. They always do this to you. They probably just want you to make something new. That's what it is. They were impressed with the little vests, and they want you to make…"

"More?"

"God, I hope not." She touched his cheek, slid her hand around the back of his neck and raked her fingers through his curls. "But it must be something like that. Don't you think?"

He held her tight. "I've always loved this dress."

"I know," she said. "And when you come home to me tonight, I'll let you wear it."

He laughed quietly into her ear.

The speaker on stage in the lodge had been presenting without the aid of a backdrop of himself magnified on the big screen. He had only a microphone, and he carried it with him as he walked back and forth on black sneakers, his sport jacket draped over the lectern. The crowd was thin, with ten or so men gathered loosely in the middle, Abe among them. The three guards who'd brought him were in a rear corner with two others, one of them Jared.

"…and chivalry, the great Ty Victor said, paraphrasing the equally great Sir Walter Scott, blends devotion to a cause, military valor, and a love of personal freedom. Who doesn't love personal freedom?" There were cheers from the meager audience, Abe included. "In the early days of chivalry, knights would fight to the death if they thought someone was a threat to their ideals or personal freedoms. Whether the threat was a man or woman didn't matter. A subversive is a subversive, and back then a subversive got a sword to the gut." He smiled. "Our ways are easier." More cheers. "Our ways are different. But they're no less honorable. 'Nothing in hate, but all in honor,' the old saying goes, and it's truer now than ever. Threat after threat pops up here," he said, with a gesture in what Abe perceived as his general direction, "pops up there…" he said, this time gesturing at a different part of the cluster as his words trailed off. He unsheathed an invisible sword and stabbed the air in front of him. "Death to traitors. 'Nothing in hate, but all in honor!'" He dropped the fake sword with a dramatic opening of his palm, pulled a real fifty-caliber Desert Eagle from the holster on his belt, and fired a shot over their heads into the far wall. After a moment of stunned motionlessness, the small crowd roared as well as a small crowd could, Abe again included.

After the presentation, when the others began breaking up to leave, Abe tried to make a casual, but quick, retreat to the exit, but Jared happened to be the guard standing by the door he'd chosen, and he was too late to pretend he hadn't seen him. Jared waved him over.

"They were really well done. Really well done." Jared's arm circled Abe's shoulder as they walked toward one of the two oversized red pickup trucks parked at the curb. "If you saw a child wearing it on the street, you'd never guess he was a walking Claymore." He laughed. "I'm not laughing at the child, Abe. Anyone who wears the vest or makes any other sacrifice in the name of the Institution of Chivalry is a hero in my book. And I'll tell you, when I showed one particular child his vest, a vest you made, he couldn't wait to put it on for his mission that, sadly, fell through." He turned to look at Abe, his arm still around him.

Abe continued looking straight ahead. "That's—That's very flattering, thank you. I'm happy you were pleased."

Four men who'd just been in the lodge with him were being guided by guards to step up into the bed of the rear pickup. A small group observing the truck from the sidewalk spit and yelled obscenities at the four in the bed taking seats on the side walls.

"Really? You don't look so happy." Jared nudged him cheerfully.

Abe smiled.

"I'm taking you to a party." Jared raised his chin at the men on the sidewalk. They lifted their chins back, then returned to their taunting. "A celebration of a recent success. We couldn't have done it without you, so of course you have to come."

"Ordinarily, I would," Abe said, "but—"

"Everyone'll be there. See?" He nodded at the red pickup sitting just feet away. "Friends of yours, I assume."

"I don't know them."

"Oh, well. That's not all of them. Some are in the first truck, and there'll be a few others. I'm sure you'll know someone." He released Abe and patted his back hard. "Whyn't you hop up." He added jovially, while tucking a thumb under his rifle sling, "Go on! Have fun."

Abe took halting steps toward the truck, then climbed in with the others. On the opposite side of the street, a group of young boys was passing by, all of them talking and gesturing at once, paying no attention to the red trucks. Abe spotted Reuben among them just as Reuben's head was starting to turn in his direction. He looked down quickly to avoid being seen.

Abe didn't look up again until the truck had reached the edge of town and was waiting at a red light to cross the intersection that had, on its far side, the rough road to the clearing. None of the other men in the truck had spoken since they'd started the journey. All eyes were on the scratched paint coating the steel ridges under their feet. When the truck stopped, they and the others from the lead pickup exited their cargo beds one at a time, the guards—including the three who'd taken Abe from his booth—having already jumped out to wait for them on the ground.

Including Abe, eleven of them marched single file as ordered to the patch of lifeless sand and rock. No weapons needed to be drawn for them to know they were being forced at gunpoint to the piece of land designated for things like this.

Others in the community who had seen the trucks roll through town also knew why they were there. Some, including Emlyn and Alek, who recognized Abe from having seen him at his booth, had followed to watch. While not everyone enjoyed what went on at the clearing, it was understood by most that to be brought there was to be unquestionably guilty of a crime against the Institution. Whether out of resignation or fear, there were no protests even among those who were saddened or disgusted by the custom. Spectators simply came to observe. Or, in some cases, to participate, but there would be no participation from the scattered audience arriving to watch today.

Abe ignored the curious onlookers, taking one forward step after another, his silence matching that of the men he was with, until they were commanded to stop and stand side by side, shoulder to shoulder. The guard with the bruise on his forehead appeared from behind them and made his way slowly down the line, stopping wordlessly in front of each man to pin a paper target over his heart. When all had been pinned, he joined his fellow guards—twelve in all—a short distance away.

Jared assessed the placement of the targets from where he was standing and nodded.

As the guards arranged themselves into a line of their own about fifteen feet from the prisoners, the shoulder to Abe's right started shaking so rapidly that it vibrated Abe's muscle. The shoulder touching his left was still. Abe directed his concentration well beyond the firing squad, all of his focus on his father's olive trees.

At Jared's "Ready," the guards raised their rifles.

The still-shouldered man on Abe's left mumbled, "Would you do it again? Whatever it was."

"Aim."

The guards rested their cheeks against their stocks as they aimed down the sights.

"Yes." Abe said, "You?"

"No question." The man's shoulder pressed Abe's as he leaned closer. "I don't know why we're practically whispering when they're going to shoot us, anyw—"

"Fire."

Sharp cracks of eleven gunshots broke the relative silence. Eleven bodies crumpled to the ground.

Blythe was sitting on the couch when Adla ran into the living room and skidded to a stop.

"Mama, why are you sitting in the dar—?"

"Go, Adla." She lightened her tone. "Go practice something new to show your dad when he comes home."

"What's wrong?"

"Oh, I'm just tired. Very, very tired. It's all right. Go on."

"Okay, but the thing I want to show him is something I always practice in the bedroom because we don't have any big walls on the roof."

"That's fine."

Adla ran off with, "I can't wait to show you and Daddy my wall flip!"

Blythe said to the living room, "We can't wait to see it, walnut."

Adla returned suddenly, running through with her sneakers. "I forgot I'm supposed to meet Ruth." She jammed her feet into her sneakers and rushed out, slamming the door to the roof stairs behind her.

Adla and Ruth were taking turns vaulting, each watching the other.

"I wish we could practice getting over the big walls," Adla said.

"Me too." Ruth effortlessly executed a perfect side vault over the small table. "How long do you think it'll take us to be as good as Emlyn?"

"Since you won't let us go back out to practice on buildings or in the park, probably a hundred years."

"For you, maybe. Anyway, Alek said not to."

Emlyn was suddenly there, climbing over Adla's parapet. She waited for Adla to finish her vault, which involved her jumping fully across the cement block and, still airborne, planting her hands on the surface behind her to propel her body forward, creating more distance before she touched ground. She landed solidly and slapped her hands together to get the grit off her fingers.

"You'll both be better than me well before a hundred years from now." Emlyn looked closely at Adla. "How are you?"

"Good. How're you?"

Emlyn watched her for another moment, then took off her scarf and cap and tucked them in her back pocket. "Adla, will you please introduce me to your mother?"

Emlyn delivered the news of Abe's execution in the dark living room after Adla had gone back out to practice with Ruth. She explained that she'd seen Abe at his booth many times, so she'd recognized him immediately as one of the men in the red truck. She told Blythe, when asked, what the man who'd led the firing squad had looked like, and Blythe had said, "Ah, yes." Emlyn told her everything she had seen, which was everything. Abe had not appeared to have been panicked. There'd been no visible delay between the gunshot and his death. No one in attendance, she lied, had cheered. The bodies had been taken away in one of the trucks and would be burned, as they all were afterward.

"Did you tell Adla any of this before coming to see me?" Blythe's voice was low and thick.

"No, Mrs. Jarvis. Of course not."

Blythe thanked her and asked her to please not say anything to Adla when she returned to the roof. Let her train, Blythe said. "I'll tell her in the morning."

The next morning, as Adla was crying alone in her room, Blythe was staring out the kitchen window over a frying pan when she thought she heard a sound in the living room. She ignored it, scooping the mass of scrambled eggs with the spatula and flipping it over. The sound came louder, this time. Knocking, followed by a frantic, "Blythe!" She slid the pan off the burner and turned off the heat before running to the living room and opening the door.

Ruth's mother Sabrina pushed inside, a cloud of pink with a casserole in her arms.

Blythe quickly closed the door behind her.

Sabrina shoved the dish at her. "I am so sorry."

Blythe brought the food to the kitchen with Sabrina following close behind. "Whisky?" She pulled the bottle from a shelf over the refrigerator.

"Well, I—I don't usually—But…But if that's what you want, I'll…Yes. Thank you."

They brought their glasses to the sunlit living room and sat on the couch.

"Can I turn off your lamp for you?"

Blythe looked at the light in the corner. It had been on all night. She shook her head.

Sabrina set her glass on the table.

Blythe cupped hers in both hands. "How did you…?" The fabric of her red dress was stretched taut over her knees. She loosened it around her legs so it would fall more modestly between her thighs. "It only just happened."

"My son."

Blythe nodded slowly. "Adla must have told Ruth."

No, Sabrina said. Reuben had shared the news with them that morning. Ruth had been surprised.

As Blythe got up and started toward the kitchen, Sabrina hurriedly added, "He didn't see—He only saw your husband being driven away."

Blythe got out a plate. "Are you hungry?" She set it on the counter and stared vacantly into the open cabinet. "I made too many eggs."

"Oh, thank you, no." Sabrina stood. "I sent Reuben on an errand so I would know exactly where he was while I visited you. He'll be home soon. I shouldn't stay."

Blythe flipped the pan of eggs upside down over the plate. "Afraid of your own son."

Silence, and then, "He's a good boy."

"I see."

"He's growing up in a much different…It's a very confusing and…I try to tell him, but he can't see my memories. He can't experience my past, or know what his father and I…This is what he knows. This." Blythe's back was still turned, her hands on the plate of eggs. Sabrina glanced at the casserole dish. "I can have Reuben bring you more tomorrow, if—"

"Thank you, but we're fine."

Sabrina started toward the door, but paused near the lamp in the living room. "Your generator. They provided it to you? I seem to remember Abe telling us that."

"Yes."

"You should…I'm sure you've thought of this, but…I think it's possible they'll be wanting it back."

"Yes," Blythe said. "Yes. Yes, they probably will. Thank you."

Sabrina slipped out into the alley.

Blythe started in the sewing room, hurriedly sweeping all of their good fabric into a garbage bag, then moved to the bedroom, where she threw all of her clothes into a suitcase. She stood in front of Abe's shirts on their hangers. She pulled out one of his favorites and wrapped it around her face and breathed it in. Before the grief could overtake her, she put it in the suitcase with her clothes. The rest of Abe's shirts and pants and jackets and shoes remained on their hangers and on the shelves he'd bolted to the closet wall.

Adla wasn't in her room, and rather than call her down to pack her suitcase, which would take far too long, Blythe did it herself, dumping in drawer after drawer of Adla's small clothes without bothering to fold them.

~

Ruth, sitting against her parapet, whisper-yelled, "My mom always says one of the best ways to help yourself when you feel sad is move."

"Move where?" Adla, her back against her own wall, wiped at the hot wetness on her cheeks and under her nose. "My mom won't want to."

"No, your body. Like the stuff we do. My mom doesn't do the stuff we do, but she walks around the house a lot."

"Oh."

"I found this site where they put up a bunch more moves. I already memorized one. We can start practicing those and surprise Emlyn."

Adla didn't say anything.

"Adla." Ruth popped her head over her wall. "Look."

When Adla pulled herself up to look over her own wall, Ruth put her fingers in her ears and stuck out her tongue. Adla smiled, then wiped her nose again. "Quit it."

"You said your dad wasn't mad when you showed him what we've been doing. You said he liked it."

"Yeah," she said, her mouth contorting with a building sob, "but he can't like it anymore."

"Still, keeping doing something he liked might make you feel better. And besides, what if he can still like things?"

Adla dried her cheeks with the heels of her hands.

"Don't you want to still show him, just in case?"

After a moment, Adla said, "Yeah."

"You should ask your mom for another computer. Tell her it's for learning."

"She doesn't like me on there. She said it's a little bit good and too much bad. She only lets me read books."

"Before Reuben got home last night I went on and—"

Adla's roof door opened. Blythe, dressed in jeans and one of Abe's shirts and with a rifle slung over her shoulder, said, "Adla has to come in now, Ruth."

Blythe presented the AR-15's magazine to Adla. "Your turn."

The weapon itself, along with Abe's Desert Eagle, a box of the handgun's forty-five caliber rounds, and the loose ammunition Blythe had just ejected from the rifle's magazine, sat between them on the living room floor. Adla took the magazine from her mother, picked up a bullet, and tried to jam it in.

"No." Blythe turned the black metal case in Adla's hand. "See that little outline of a bullet on the side? That's the direction they should face."

Holding the magazine to her stomach for support with one hand, she struggled against the spring with the other until a sturdy click announced the proper seating of the round.

"Ten more," Blythe said.

"Why?"

"Because this is what boys your age are learning."

Adla picked up another bullet.

With her elbows on the counter for support, Adla aimed the rifle out the kitchen window. "Like this?"

Blythe adjusted the position of the stock and one of Adla's elbows. "Cheek touching. Good. Butt," she said, feeling beneath Adla's collar bone to confirm it was nestled as well as it could be in Adla's shoulder pocket, "good. Now, once you find your target," she said, tapping the front sight, "keep your focus here."

"I don't get it." Adla swung the gun toward Blythe as she turned. "Why—"

Blythe pushed the barrel away. "Adla! Never, never, never point a gun, loaded or unloaded, in the direction of any living thing you don't intend to kill." She took the rifle from her daughter and led her back to the living room, where stray rounds and their empty cardboard boxes were still on the floor. "We'll practice more later. Help me clean this up, and then I want you to show me where your hiding place is."

Adla slumped to the floor and scooped bullets together.

"How big is it?" Blythe said. "Can two people fit?"

Adla shrugged.

Blythe sat next to her on the rug. "I'm going to tell you something, and I want you to try your best to not think about it once I tell you. Don't ask questions," she said, helping return bullets to the boxes, "don't use your imagination, and don't be afraid. Just listen to what I say, and understand that what I say is simply the way things are. Do you understand?"

"Uh-huh."

Blythe touched Adla's hair, in need of another cut, and, without any effort to soften a reality that could not be softened, explained that the group of people who had given them the generator were the same group of people who were responsible for Adla's father's death. The generator had been for his use, she said, and now that he wasn't using it, anymore, she assumed they would want it back. She would leave the garage door open so they could get it without needing anyone to give them access, but she suspected they would want to come inside the house.

"Why?" Adla said.

She and Abe hadn't told Adla what they did for the government, and they had resolved to never, ever tell her what they'd been asked to do toward the end. "I don't...I don't really know, walnut. Maybe to take our things, or maybe to punish me. They were mad at him for something, and it's possible they're mad at me, too, because I'm his wife. They might only take the generator and go, and we won't have to worry about any of this. But if they want to come in, we need them to think we don't live here, anymore. So we're going to hide. Do you understand?"

Adla nodded.

"Is there room in your hiding spot for both of us?"

Adla nodded.

"All right. Finish cleaning this up."

The last thing to do was store their suitcases. It wouldn't do to put them in a closet, where they would surely look, so it would have to be the roof. Blythe lugged both suitcases up the stairs and shoved them through the door and looked around. There was nowhere to hide them. The best she could do was set them beside the door near the hinges so the door would, ideally, block them from view when it opened. She was stacking them into place when she heard, behind her, "Psst."

Ruth was standing a few feet away from the edge of her own rooftop. She waved.

"Hi, sweetie," Blythe whispered.

"Are you hiding those?"

"Trying."

"I think they'll find them there."

"Oh, I don't think they'll even come up here. I'm sure it'll be fine."

"But what if they do, Mrs. Jarvis?"

Blythe raised her arms hopelessly.

Ruth held up her index finger and ran inside. When she returned less than a minute later, her mother was behind her.

Sabrina pointed at the suitcases, then beckoned toward herself with both hands.

"She wants you to toss them over," Ruth said.

"Really?"

Sabrina nodded and beckoned again. Blythe picked up a suitcase.

"Wait!" Ruth crept to the parapet and peered over, checking left and right. She gave the OK sign, and Blythe tossed the first suitcase across the alley. It landed with a thud, freezing all three of them wide-eyed. When many seconds passed without anyone below calling out to them or, alternatively, getting suspiciously quiet, Ruth went to the wall again. She signed another OK, and Blythe heaved the second suitcase over.

The next day, Blythe was periodically looking out the window while folding a short stack of clothes on the kitchen counter when she saw a red pickup truck park on the street in front of their house. Two young guards immediately flung open their doors and jumped out of the cab.

Blythe grabbed the clothes and ran out of the kitchen, clutching them as she searched room to room. "Adla," she whispered. "Adla!"

On their respective rooftops, Adla and Ruth were strength training.

"I don't know," Adla said quietly while at the bottom of a decline pushup, her feet up on the cement block, "when I would ever use a fraction."

Ruth came up from an elevated squat, a brick in each hand. "When you have to measure cream or sugar or yeast or—"

"Ugh." Adla pushed up, lowered down. "My mom tried to make me bake, and—"

The door to the roof flew open. Blythe grabbed Adla around the waist and hoisted her to her feet. "It's now," she whispered across to Ruth. "Tell your mother." She whisked Adla inside.

Blythe and Adla sat in complete darkness. The only sound was their breathing. "We're listening for the generator rolling out of the garage," Blythe whispered. "And then their truck leaving. Once the truck leaves, we're—"

THUD. THUD. THUD.

Blythe and Adla jumped at the pounding on the door, making one of them noisily nudge the rifle at their feet. Blythe felt around and snatched it up and set it in her lap. "No more moving," she said as quietly as she could into Adla's ear.

"It wasn't m—"

"Shhh."

The next loud noise wasn't a dull thud, but the thin, cracking sound of the door being kicked in.

Adla and Blythe could only listen from their secret place in the dark. First it was muffled voices, the words unintelligible, but the guards were soon close enough to hear.

"…might be more vests. Look around."

"I'll go left, you go right.—Didn't he have a wife?"

"Yeah. Think so."

"Look for guns, too. He didn't have one on him."

A faint, high-pitched whistle rose, fell. Rose, fell.

Blythe put her hand on Adla's arm and followed it up to her shoulder, then her neck. She guided Adla's head until it was touching her own and put her lips directly on Adla's ear and whispered, "Breathe through your mouth, walnut."

The whistling stopped.

Their footsteps came closer. Blythe held Adla to her.

"Nothing in there." Scuffling, and something being slid to the side. "Hey, I tell you about last week? Hooo! Eleven. Still think about that one. Nice, nice, nice."

There was no reply.

"Got a problem?"

"It's young."

"Pff. Ain't nothin' but a girl. Brains of a child at any age, anyway. You know they stop developing at ten, or something like that? At least, up here." He laughed. "Personally, I liked the one at thirteen best. They get too young and they're too damn small and wiry. Like fucking a starving dog, all stiff and—"

"Biting you, I hope."

"Skeet gave her to Rhodes for his guys—the eleven, not the thirteen—so she's fifty miles away, now. You should try it. Ever been to the top floor in the shack?"

"No."

"They keep 'em up there before they pass 'em on. Not just little ones. All ages." He laughed. "Wait, naw, not all ages." He made a gagging sound. "Anyway, talk to Skeet."

"There's nothing here."

"Hey. Check this out."

"It's a sock."

"A female sock. Where d'you think she is?"

"Not here. Wherever she is, she won't last, guns or no. Either way, not our problem. Let's get what we came for."

Blythe and Adla stayed hidden through the sound of grit grinding under the generator's wheels, shouts about where to position it to roll it up the wood plank ramps, and the slamming of the truck's doors. When at last the pickup's rumbling engine faded to silence, they came out.

The kitchen door had been left open. Blythe checked the windows for anyone lurking, saw no one, and closed it.

"Hello?" Sabrina's voice was coming from the living room. "Blythe? Your door was, was open, so I…"

Blythe sent Adla to her room and joined Sabrina, first closing the door to the alley. The frame had been damaged, but the latch worked. They sat on the couch.

Sabrina said, "I don't think they'll be back. What do they care about some empty house?"

"That's my hope."

"Well." She pressed her hands into her lap. "I wanted to be sure you were both safe after their visit."

Blythe thanked her for that, as well as for storing their suitcases.

"Oh, it's no trouble. You've never met anyone less curious about what's in their own home than Reuben and Stewart. Not that Stewart would take issue. Anyway, I also wanted… Well…"

"Yes?"

It came out in a rush: Stewart had lost his job months before and had no other prospects. They needed to make money. They still had a generator, and Abe's booth was just sitting there. Maybe Stewart could work it?

"It's difficult having them both home." Sabrina's knee bounced under the drape of pink fabric covering her from her shoulders to her ankles. She tucked her thick brown hair behind her ears. "Reuben is so critical of his father for not working. He's getting worse, Reuben is. Militant. There are so many halfway decent ones that I don't know why he's not seeing those others for what they are, but something about it…It has a hold on him. What I'm trying to say is that I— Blythe, I don't have nearly the skills you do. Stewart could make the sales, we thought, by taking over the booth, and we—he would buy the fabric and other essentials, but he'd want you to do the sewing, if you…Oh, but he would pay you, of cour—"

"Yes."

THREE YEARS LATER

Emlyn observed from the cement block on Adla's rooftop as Adla and Ruth trained under moonlight. Several stunts into a series of intermediate-level ground exercises, Ruth came up against her parapet. She winked at Adla, then swung over the dwarf wall and clung to it for a fraction of a second before dropping into the alley. Quickly, she hopped onto her dad's booth and leaped from it as high as she could, using inertia, her feet, and a strong grip on the top of the wall to climb back onto her own roof.

"When did…?" Emlyn stood.

"Right after you and Alek leave," Ruth said.

"We always watched until you got around the corner and we knew you wouldn't be coming back." Adla went to the far edge of her own rooftop, turned around, and ran across it. She planted one foot on the ledge of her wall and used the forward motion combined with her own strength to propel her over the alley, then touched down with the other foot on the ledge of Ruth's wall and slowed herself with a showboating roll on the rooftop. "I learned this as fast as I could so I could get over here when me and mom had to hide but I didn't have time to get into our spot," she explained.

"We're sorry we kept it from you," Ruth said. "But we were afraid you'd stop coming. You said you'd never come back if we weren't safe."

Emlyn was smiling. "At this point," she said, "I don't think there's anything else I can teach you that you can't figure out for yourselves."

"There is," Adla said. "We want you to teach us to get around. Out there."

"We want to do what you do," Ruth said. "We only ever stay right here, so maybe we can drop down and climb up in this exact spot, and we can get across, but that's it. We never leave. We're so bored."

"Alek thought it would be at least another year until you asked." Emlyn covered her nose and mouth with her scarf and tucked her long hair inside her cap. "Go get changed."

From that night on, two times a week and month after month for the next three and a half years, Emlyn and Alek led Adla and Ruth, dressed fully in black, down alleys dark with shadows. They taught them to run up walls from the ground with no obstacles to assist them. They brought them to abandoned houses and trained them to cat-claw to high window ledges and from there to higher window ledges to rooftops, one after another to improve their stamina and endurance. They had them practice all of the ground escape maneuvers—vaults, rolls, leaps, climbs—in the sport park, when possible, and coached them on how to jump off higher and higher platforms.

On the evening of one of their periodic visits to the top of the lodge, the town's tallest structure, Emlyn asked as she always did whether Adla and Ruth had, in the days leading up to the drop, been doing enough training on their own from shorter heights to focus on form and keep their muscles strong.

Yes, they said. Yes, yes, and could they please jump, now? They both loved the exercise and were impatient because they were only allowed on the building when accompanied by Emlyn and Alek.

The lodge had a street out front but an empty lot behind it, making it the best location for high-dropping and rolling. Grass would have been better, softer, but unless they happened to find their way to a different part of the country, grass wasn't what they would land on if they ever did have to jump off a tall building. That someone was always in the lodge was the only drawback, but the four of them were always careful to climb up the side that stayed dark at night, then stay on the parapet's ledge to avoid the possibility of having their footsteps heard through the ceiling by someone in a room below. And because the assumption was that everyone was too scared to get near the lodge unless they belonged there, patrols around the building were light, if unnervingly sporadic.

Ruth was up first, and Emlyn offered her no pointers. At this stage of their training, comments, when there were any, were saved for the end-of-night debrief under the olive tree.

"Bye," Ruth said. She bent her knees slightly, jumped, and a little over a second later gave her feet only enough time to touch the ground before rolling forward on one of her shoulders, popping up, and walking a few steps out of the way. Emlyn and Alek gave her a thumbs-up.

"See ya," Adla said, her form as she left the rooftop identical to Ruth's. Her landing was less successful. When her feet hit ground, her balance was thrown off and she fell hard into the roll. Her "Ugh!" was unintentional and loud.

A light turned on, its warm yellow beam falling on the asphalt not far from where Adla lay. Ruth hurried over and helped her up and dragged her into the dark. Emlyn and Alek jumped off the building and caught up with them, Emlyn taking the lead and instructing them to follow her. Moving more slowly than she ordinarily would to accommodate Adla, she led them to a nearby driveway behind a warped, blue metal fence where they squatted in a tight huddle.

Alek whispered, "They probably didn't hear anything. It was just someone getting up to go to the bathroom."

Emlyn, her attention on the other side of the fence, put her finger to her lips. Seconds later, she pointed out at the street where two guards were marching back-to-back, rifles pointed outward.

"Fine," Alek mouthed, rolling his eyes.

Emlyn's laugh was a hard breath through her nose.

They waited for the guards to pass. At Emlyn's signal, they made their way to the intersection at the edge of town and ran wide of the clearing toward the olive trees.

They were breathless when they arrived. Caps and scarves came off as soon as they sat down, with Emlyn close enough to Alek for their arms to touch. Adla took off her sneakers and rubbed her heels through black socks.

"Bad landing," Alek said.

"Yeah, but I was good all those other times." Adla put a shoe on.

"You need to have your toes out."

"They were."

"No," Emlyn said, "they weren't."

"I forgot," Adla said. "I'll practice more."

Emlyn watched her put on her other sneaker. "You can probably practice in daylight if you want to, can't you?" She lifted her hair off her neck, damp with sweat. "I should cut my hair short like yours. Look, there's hardly any sweat on her face, even after running—and hurt!—from the guards."

"I sweat enough."

"She goes out during the day. Alone. I've seen you. Wearing a shirt and shorts instead of that ugly pink sheet with sleeves." Emlyn took a packet of crackers from her pocket. "The first time I saw you, you were coming out of the grocery store. It was a few months ago." She pulled out a cracker, then passed the package to Ruth. "You looked so comfortable with it that at first I swore it wasn't you. The hair, the clothes, the way you...stood there, with this look on your face like you owned the street. I thought, 'It can't be her. It's just some boy who looks a lot like her.' But then two little kids playing tag headed straight for you, and the way you avoided them, the way your body moved...I've seen the way you move for nine years. I knew it was you."

"My mom needs me," Adla said. "I have to."

"'Have to'?" Emlyn gestured for Adla to take a cracker and pass the rest on. "I didn't even know it was possible to do something like that. I mean, I never even thought about it. And you've been doing it all this time. You've been totally and completely free. 'Have to'? You should be out there doing anything you want every chance you get."

Alek said, "Emlyn."

"I would, if I looked like that instead of this." Emlyn comically stuck out her chest and puckered her lips. "No one even notices you, do they?"

"I'm careful, so not really." Adla passed the crackers to Ruth. "Except you, I guess."

"Lucky. Lucky, lucky, lucky." She said, "Is it hard?"

"I don't know," Adla said. "I guess not. If I'm flattened out and in the right clothes, I don't even think about it, really."

"What's it like? Do you like it?"

"Emlyn."

"*Alek.*"

Adla said she'd been doing it for so long she was used to it.

"What if you couldn't do it anymore? Would you be mad?"

Adla laughed. "Yeah."

Quiet fell. Much of the town was dark but for a few dim points of window light, and the stars were thick and bright.

"'Pour me out a potion,'" Alek recited softly, "'to drink her soft, sweet kisses. I suffer drought. Healing is drinking from her moist, fresh lips.'" He raised his eyebrows at Emlyn. "'But she is content without me.'"

"Utterly." Emlyn smiled at him. He pinched her arm.

Ruth looked adoringly at Alek and gave him the plastic sleeve she'd had sitting in her lap. "That was beautiful."

"Thank you, Ruth." He slid a cracker in his mouth.

"Oh, no." Emlyn waved her hand. "First of all, it's not beautiful. He's blaming a poor, innocent woman for his suffering. Second, don't give Alek the credit. It belongs to some poet."

"Bashar ibn Burd," Alek said, "and rumor has it that he was ugly. So, maybe she didn't want him. But I don't think he's blaming her for anything. I think he just loves her."

Ruth sighed.

"I think I love this spot," Adla said.

"Wait, no. Just a second. Adla, you and Ruth need to know this stuff. Alek may not see it, but he couldn't—you, Alek, couldn't be more wrong about what he's saying in that poem. It's attitudes like that—'Oh, poor victimized me, the cruel, cold woman doesn't want me'—that have me drowning in the pink frock from hell until I turn forty and have to switch to that dingy gray muumuu, if I survive that long. Your kind," she said, "is a bunch of weak nut-sacks so afraid of being hurt or challenged by women that the only way you could feel big and strong was to beat us into submission."

"True," Alek said. "My kind did do that. But only because you're all so scary."

Emlyn, laughing, swatted him on the shoulder.

"My dad wasn't like that," Adla said quietly.

"I'm sure he wasn't." Emlyn's voice was tender. "There are probably more like him than we know. There have to be. But a lot of them are afraid to be different even if they want to be, because if they're found out, they're punished for it. If there's anything these government men hate and fear more than big, bad women, it's brave men like your dad and Alek."

Adla circled her arms around her legs and rested her chin on her knees. Wind pushed at the branches of her grandpa's olive tree, rustling the leaves. She said, "I meant it when I said I love it here."

Emlyn kissed Alek's cheek and said she did, too.

Alek gave what was left of the crackers back to Emlyn. "Me, too."

Ruth piped, "So do I."

Adla crept down the hall from her bedroom holding her father's Desert Eagle at the ready. When she reached the entry to the living room, she took a step past the door frame, rotated into the room, and aimed at a circle target taped to the wall. She tucked the handgun into the waist of her pants and jumped into a front flip, landing in the space she'd cleared earlier by sliding the couch against the wall. As soon as her feet touched the floor, she yanked out the weapon and took aim again.

"Adla," Blythe said from the kitchen.

Adla looked over her shoulder at her mother, who was moving things around in the cabinet.

"I need you to go to the store."

In her bedroom, Adla pulled her new binder over her chest and checked herself in the mirror, then put on a t-shirt and looked again. Flat enough to pass for a boy, and finally comfortable. When her breasts had started developing she'd tried everything from surgical bandages to wrapping herself in duct tape, and she had always ended up itchy, in pain, or afraid when, as had happened once or twice, her homemade binding had started to fail before she'd made it home. The idea to use Ruth's house as an address to receive packages had come late, but at least it had come. Eventually she would have to ask Ruth and her mother to accept the delivery of a stick-on beard, but for now she was still young enough to get away with not having facial hair. She and her mother had yet to figure out what she would do in the years she was expected to have patchy stubble.

Dressed in denim shorts and a dark t-shirt, Adla walked into town while watching for Reuben as she always did, lifted her chin in greeting when she entered the store, gathered the items on her mother's short list, and set the basket on the counter.

The store owner was the same man she had been buying from for the last five years. He had taken over after his father died. Like his father, Elmer had strangely pink cheeks. Also like his father, he showed contempt for girls and women accompanied by the men in his aisles. Unlike his father, though, he didn't ignore them but would put on a scowl or a sneer or a glare that would sit heavy on his face until he knew the target of his repulsion had seen it. Only then would he relax the muscles around his eyes and mouth.

But he was always nice to Adla. Or, as he knew her, Addie.

"She should figure out what the hell she wants and send you for one big trip 'stead of having you come out here three times a week for this and that." He rang up a container of minced onion and dropped it in a red plastic bag.

"'Send' me?" Adla gave him her best eyebrows. "She doesn't 'send' me for shit. I have to eat her cooking, so I damn well better like it."

He laughed. "The simple things do try, though. You gotta give 'em that." He rang up her paper towels and added them to the bag.

Through the window behind Elmer, Adla noticed a young man walking on the sidewalk across the street with his shoulders raised self-consciously, his eyes downcast. She must have taken too obvious an interest, because Elmer turned to look, too. They both watched the unusual specimen cross the street toward the store.

"That's one strange-looking boy." Still looking out the window, Elmer put Adla's coffee filters in the bag.

The figure came closer, and Adla's breath caught.

"Face smooth as a baby's," Elmer said. "Something's funny 'bout—"

"Hey, now." Adla dropped change on the counter, getting his attention off the window and on her. "Have a heart for late bloomers." She rubbed her cheeks and chin.

"Consider yourself lucky," he said.

Elmer swept the change into his palm along with the bills Adla had laid on top. She rubbed her chin one more time and shot a finger-gun at him for good measure, then took her time walking out of the store. Once on the sidewalk, she hurried after Emlyn, whose short red hair half a block away was even easier to spot than her awkward gait. Adla was relieved when Emlyn stopped at a fruit stand on the corner, but the vendor looked twice at her as she selected an apple from the basket. Adla watched her set it back down, say something to him, and smile at him before walking away.

"Don't do that," Adla muttered under her breath. "Don't smile."

But the vendor didn't seem to have been bothered by it. Adla kept an eye on him, waiting for him to either signal another man to follow Emlyn or close his booth and do it himself, but all he did was move the apple she'd set down until he found a better spot for it. Adla dismissed him as a danger and looked for Emlyn.

She was gone.

Adla followed the same general direction Emlyn had been going and, not seeing her bright hair anywhere, turned onto a side street where she knew there were a few stands and an industrial sized waste bin allowing easy access to rooftops. As she always had, she looked up when trying to find her mentor, careful to stay out of the way of people on the street, but she didn't see her anywh—

"Boo!" Emlyn jumped out from behind the bin, making Adla drop her bag. Emlyn giggled and picked up the minced onion that had rolled out. "You're terrible at following."

"You're terrible at being a man," Adla whispered, dropping the plastic container in the bag and wrapping the handle around her wrist. "If you were better at it I wouldn't have been following you in the first place."

"You don't like my hair?" Emlyn reached up and ran her fingers through it. "I tried to make it as even as I could."

Two guards rounded the corner at the far end of the side street and were coming their way, but Adla and Emlyn, standing on the opposite side of the large trash bin, didn't see them.

"Your hair is fine." Adla scratched her own chin as if there were a beard there. "But you need more of it." She nodded a greeting at a trio of men passing by.

"It's fine. No one's noticed. I think they think I'm a teenager." Emlyn smiled.

"And stop smiling," Adla whispered. "It makes you look like a girl." She studied Emlyn's chest. "How in the world did you do that?"

Emlyn winced for effect. "Well, I can't breathe, so whatever I did, I think I did it wrong."

Adla laughed at the same moment the guards came into view several feet behind the bin. She whispered, "Come—"

"Watch this. In broad daylight, just like you and Alek." Taking advantage of a clearing in pedestrian traffic, Emlyn stepped out and walked behind a couple of young men, swaying her torso in an impressive, swaggering imitation of the one on the right. She looked back at Adla and laughed.

When she faced forward again, Emlyn was too late to avoid bumping hard into a man who had been deep in conversation and paying no attention. The impact startled an "Oh!" out of her.

One of the guards narrowed his eyes at her. His gaze then dropped down.

Adla looked where he was looking and saw the problem. Emlyn's homemade binding had released her. The shirt she had chosen, probably one of Alek's, had fit loosely enough around a flattened chest, but the fabric now strained at the buttons.

Emlyn noticed it, too, and bounded—despite how running made her shirt move—away from the guards marching toward her. She leaped onto a wall and used a foot to push off, almost making it past the guards when one of them spun around and swung his rifle's butt stock into her knee. She cried out with a distinctly feminine voice and dropped. The two guards closed in.

Emlyn scrambled, kicking at the guards' grasping hands until she was free and running, running, past Adla and toward the busy street.

"Anyone who doesn't stop that—that *woman*—will get the same punishment she does," one of the guards shouted.

All of the men close enough to have heard the threat, as well as the few women who were with them, crowded the exit to the main road, blocking Emlyn's access. She headed for a narrow window ledge on a building at the corner. Under the window was a ceramics booth with no one manning it. Emlyn jumped onto it, and the guards came for her. She leaped off before they could touch her and reached high for the window ledge. A hand suddenly gripped her ankle tight, and the ledge got farther away as she was jerked out of the air.

Emlyn hit the ground flat on her back. Adla waited for one of the gathered men to say something that would save her. No one did.

The guards lifted Emlyn harshly by her arms. One of them faced her away and zip-tied her wrists behind her back while the other held her. Adla saw a spreading spot on the back of Emlyn's head that was redder than her hair. The guards shouted and waved at the crowd they'd gathered, ordering them to move, get out of the way.

Adla followed from a distance, as did many others. Some were quiet like her. Others raged, pumping their fists and screaming, their faces pink and bright, spit spilling over red lips. As more and more people fell in from the streets in the push toward the edge of town, Adla was forced bit by bit to the back until all she could see were the heads of the mob in front of her. Still, she followed, crossing with the rest of them when they got to the last intersection, stepping over rocks and brush she could navigate with her eyes closed, and stopping in the spot she'd been taught to stay clear of.

The crowd started to thin as it shaped itself into a circle surrounding a patch of soft sand, and Adla was able to get close enough to see. In the center, the two guards were forcing Emlyn to her knees. She went down without struggling and looked out at the people. Adla stepped through two tall men to stand up front, her red bag held in front of her.

It didn't take long for Emlyn to find her. She looked at Adla with eyes that were bright and alive in a way Adla had never seen them. And even as one of the guards launched into a statement—"Under most circumstances, we'd do this in the morning after a fair review. We are, above all else, fair in our treatment of all men and all women. But you're not a man, are you, and we can all see that you clearly don't want to be a woman…"—Emlyn's mouth curled, on just one side, into the faintest of smiles.

The men circled around her began picking up the rocks at their feet. Adla scanned their faces frantically, looking for at least one showing shock over the proceedings and the will to try to stop what was happening. What she saw instead was impatience, satisfaction, delight, and the impassive gaze of fearful disagreement.

"…a woman dresses like a man, she is denying her true and natural role. She also presumes to be mentally equipped and otherwise entitled to enjoy the natural rights of men. She is, therefore, an abomination." He stepped in front of Emlyn and looked down at her. "Do you understand?"

Emlyn's eyes shined, and her back was tall and straight. She said nothing.

The guard looked over his shoulder at his partner, who rolled his eyes and shrugged.

"So be it." He turned and, with his partner, stepped out of the way.

Without thinking, Adla started forward, but Emlyn corrected her with a warning stare. Adla stayed where she was.

Emlyn took in the spectators, her eyes stopping somewhere to Adla's right. Adla craned her neck to peer through the bodies and saw that Emlyn had found Alek. He was fixated on her, unmoved by the yelling around him and the jostling of his body every time someone bent down to pick up or exchange a stone. He was crying, something Adla knew only because the light hit a tear on his cheek just right.

Emlyn mouthed, "It's okay," and smiled lovingly at him.

He returned the smile.

Emlyn looked at Adla. She subtly jerked her chin—*Go*—and returned her attention to Alek. Through the first rock flung, a miss by at least two feet, she didn't flinch, but kept her eyes steady on Alek, whose concentration on her didn't waver. Adla backed through the crowd until she couldn't see anything, until she would no longer be a third wheel in their final moments together, but she couldn't, wouldn't, stop herself from hearing the crack of the stones that made contact, or the dull thudding sound they made when they fell from Emlyn's body to the earth.

Adla watched the men's faces through burning tears. They were somehow smiling even as they raged, their skin flushed and sparkling with excited sweat, their bodies moving not in unison but in concert with each other in some primal animal rhythm.

All but one, that was. Reuben, standing far enough back to be visible to Adla but surely close enough to see Emlyn, was turning a rock over and over in his hand. Next to him, men pantomimed throwing, urging him on. One of them nudged him with a shoulder as if to push him forward. Reuben shook his head and gestured toward the others. *No, no*, his gesturing said. *It's their turn. I'll wait.* He started coughing, then, and dropped the rock to put his hands to his mouth. Coughing and coughing, he backed through the bodies until Adla could no longer see him.

She stayed until the last rock was thrown.

Adla hadn't seen Alek leave, but he had probably gone when there was no denying Emlyn was dead. Adla was the only one there when they came to take the body. She watched, tossing and catching a rock and fighting back anything that would give her away, as they loaded Emlyn's limp figure into the back of one of their red pickup trucks.

Adla had been gone for two hours on an errand that should have taken half an hour, and Blythe had just come downstairs from her fourth trip to the roof to scan the alley for her when Adla burst through the living room door and slammed it behind her.

"Adla!" Blythe took the red bag Adla thrust in her hand as she passed. "What took you so long?" She followed her to her room, but Adla mumbled, "I need to be alone," and closed the door.

That night, they sat in the living room over empty plates after a quiet dinner Blythe had had to coax her to eat. Adla's eyes were plump and narrow from hours of crying.

"She was the one who always told us to be careful," Adla said. "She wasn't careful at all! She did something she had to know was—She was as bad as Dad. Why didn't he just do what they told him? Why did he do something he knew would get him killed? Why is everyone so stupid?"

"Your father was anything but stupid."

"Why, then?"

"Adla. You of all people are asking this? Why do you go outside at night to run around in the dark, knowing how dangerous it is? Do you know how much sleep I haven't had in the last three years? Why do you think I never said anything?—It's a real question. I'd like you to answer."

"Because…I don't know."

"Then think."

"I don't know!"

Blythe stacked the plates and walked them into kitchen. "I used to try to stop you from doing things I thought were—"

"When you thought I was wasting time."

"No." She set the plates on the counter and returned to the couch. "Not wasting time, walnut. Living for the wrong world. From the beginning, when you were still very young, you didn't listen. I thought…When I decided you should be free to be who you were, I told myself it was because I wanted you to be happy. And it was true. But I also realized that if you were going to keep doing those things you were doing, you had to be as good as you could possibly be. I couldn't let you be distracted by being afraid of me when you had people a lot more dangerous than your mother to hide from. You had to, and you have to, focus only on what's happening around you when you're out there, on staying safe."

"Maybe I don't deserve to be safe."

Blythe curled a finger under Adla's chin and turned her head, forcing her to look at her. "Pardon me?"

"Emlyn cut her hair off because of me. She was out there joking around like an idiot and—Because of me. If I could go back in time and stop her, I would. If you said right now that I could never leave the house again until I got married, I'd do it. I might never get married, but I guess that just means I'd never leave the house, either."

"Why would I say that? It makes no sense. How would that save Emlyn?"

"It wouldn't. But I don't know, maybe it would save me. Maybe it's just smart."

"And how would we get our groceries?" Blythe smiled and touched Adla's short bangs.

Adla shrugged like the child she used to be.

"If you really wanted to do that," Blythe said, "you would already have made the decision for yourself. And though I can indeed at least try to lock you up in this house for the rest of your life, I won't."

"Why? Why won't you save me? Why didn't you save him when you knew he would die?"

Blythe closed her eyes. "Adla."

"I'm sorry. I didn't mean—"

Blythe took Adla's hands. "Walnut, everybody dies. Everybody. The man who led your father to his death will die, if he isn't dead already. Whoever it was who killed Emlyn will die. You will die. I will die. No matter what. Nothing anyone does can stop that. Do you understand?"

"No," she sniffed.

"Every time you leave this house, I'm scared to death. When you run errands for me, I can stand in the same spot for an hour and not know how much time has passed while I'm waiting for you to come home. At night, because you're so good now at coming and going without me hearing you, I never look in your room, anymore, because I have to pretend you're safe in bed if I want to get any sleep at all. I am terrified of something happening to you, Adla. But the only thing that scares me more than the thought of someday losing you is the thought of you being unhappy. Your father could have lived to be an old man if he'd done what he was told, but he would have hated himself. And you might have learned to hate him for it too, over time."

"No, I wouldn't."

"Well. That's what you say now in the spirit of petulance, but you'll realize later, when you've given it some thought, that I'm right. My point, Adla, is—"

"Why didn't he already hate himself? You said he was already giving them vests—"

"*We* were giving them vests. And do you know, Adla, it's considered impolite to refer to things someone might once have foolishly revealed while under the influence."

"Okay. But still, that was way before the kid vests, you said. That wasn't enough to hate himself? Weren't people still dying?"

Those who had worn the adult vests they'd made, Blythe said, had been old enough to make the difficult decision to push, or not push, the detonator's button and suffer the consequences of either choice. Children weren't old enough to make that decision.

"But people still died," Adla said.

"Yes. You can't save everyone." Blythe patted her leg. "Your father died early, but he had no regrets about who he was or how he lived his life. I have a feeling the same is true for your friend Emlyn." She invited a now-crying Adla into her arms and stroked her back. "You'll do whatever is right for you, my love, whether that means continuing to enjoy the freedom you've created for yourself, or being a prisoner in your own home. But only you can decide."

Alek was already sitting beneath the olive tree when Adla and Ruth arrived that night.

"I thought you'd come," he said.

The girls sat cross-legged side by side, facing him.

"You're leaving," Ruth said.

Alek nodded, and Ruth looked down, away, anywhere but at Alek. He said, "She always said if anything happened to her I should 'make the rounds.'" He picked up rocks and sand and let it fall. "She didn't want to be gone without a goodbye."

At the same time, Adla and Ruth said, "I didn't want her to be gone at all."

Alek rested the back of his head against the tree.

They were all quiet for a while.

"Where will you go?" Ruth finally said.

"Anywhere else."

At the sound of footsteps, they all turned. Alek nodded a greeting at a figure in black swaying toward them. Her hair was dark, and short like Adla's, so she didn't bother to cover it with a hood.

"Adla, Ruth," Alek said, "Emlyn's cousin, Carla. She lives on top of the liquor store."

Carla reached out and shook hands. To Alek she said, "Did you see it happen?"

Adla stole a look at Alek. He shook his head no.

"I wish I'd seen it," Carla said. "I'd find whoever did it and kill him back."

"Me, too," Ruth said. "I would."

Carla said, "I'd shoot him right between the eyes."

Alek settled his head on the tree again and looked off into the dark. "She'd still be dead."

Adla could picture it, this wiry girl in clothes blacker than shadows slinking around corners, climbing through windows, and sneaking down hallways until she found him, took careful aim at his head, shot him until he was dead, and dissolved into the night.

But, unlike Adla, Carla didn't know what he looked like.

Adla strapped the rifle across her back and turned side to side in the mirror. The binder kept the sling from digging between her breasts and giving her away, even in a t-shirt.

When only the booth workers were below, she made a running leap over the alley with her spare binder in her hand. It was her first roof-hop carrying things. She lost nothing, and the weapon wasn't too uncomfortable on the landing and hadn't shifted much. She took it off and propped it against the wall near the door's hinges, then lifted the back of her shirt to tuck the binder into her waistband before opening the rooftop door.

She stopped halfway down the stairs to listen for Reuben's voice, as she always did, even though he had always been out somewhere doing something any time she'd visited.

Sabrina opened the door at the bottom of the stairwell and, looking down, reached in for a pair of Ruth's shoes sitting on a lower step.

"Hi, Mrs. Larsen," Adla said.

"Oh!" Sabrina's hands flew up and the sneakers dropped. "Didn't Ruth tell you it's safe to use the downstairs door after nine?"

"She did, but I…I don't want to make your husband have to pretend to Reuben that I—"

"Stewart is a grown man, Adla." She gathered up the shoes. "Reuben has his faults, we all know what they are, and we all work around them. I think Stewart would like it if you said hi, now and then." She stepped back to let Adla pass. "She's in her room." She gave Adla the sneakers. "Please tell her to stop leaving them on the stairs."

Lengths of dark hair covered the towels on Ruth's bedroom floor. Adla stepped back with the scissors Ruth had taken from the kitchen and told her to turn her head left, then right.

"It's still not too late," Adla said. "You don't have to go with me."

"What do you think Emlyn would think?" Ruth said, evaluating her haircut in the mirror.

Adla thought for a moment. "I don't know. But I think Alek would say not to do it."

"I meant about my hair."

Adla brushed fine clippings off Ruth's shoulders. "I shouldn't have told you."

"But we tell each other everything. And anyway, I invited myself. I loved her too, you know." Ruth pulled at some hairs on her head until they stretched the full inch and a half. "I don't think my parents'll believe me if I say I cut off all my hair because of a teenage crisis. What if I say it's because I'm upset because my friend died?"

Adla stopped with the scissors. "I don't think you should use her like that."

"But it's true."

"Not the way you'd be saying it."

Ruth slumped in her chair. "I don't want it to be true in any way."

"Sit straight." Adla trimmed a section at the base of Ruth's neck. "People always think teenagers are having a crisis. They'll believe you."

"My mom'll still lecture me when she sees it."

Adla reminded Ruth that that was why they had planned their exit so that Ruth was sneaking out with the gun, and Adla was the one who would have to walk past Sabrina. The lecture could come later. "When does she get you for dinner?"

"She doesn't. I come out at four-thirty so Reuben can quiz me before we eat."

"We're on matrimony, right?"

"Yeah, but…Why are you reading that stuff? I thought you stopped."

"My mom makes me. Just in case." Adla looked sternly at Ruth in the mirror. "And what are the five pillars of being a good wife, young lady?"

Ruth shook a finger at her. "Surely you mean being a good woman, Miss Jarvis."

"Why, they are one and the same, aren't they?"

"Yes, I should say they are."

"Very well. Go on, Miss Larsen."

"Okay." She closed her eyes, serious now. "First is…is praise him?"

"Oh, yes, praise him on high. 'Gosh, you are just the best at everything. How do you do everything so impressively, so superiorly?'"

"'And you're so strong.'"

"'And so smart. The smartest!'"

"'And, of course…'"

"'Huge!'"

They laughed.

When Ruth didn't continue, Adla pressed her to. Reuben would be annoyed about her hair, but if she didn't know her material, he would also be suspicious.

"Always put myself second," Ruth said, using her fingers to count off, "work hard at being attrac…tive…" She made a face at the mirror.

"Just because they like long hair doesn't mean short hair isn't attractive."

"But they look at us funny when we have short hair."

"If they don't like seeing it, they should lock us up at home. Oh, wait."

Ruth laughed and went on. "Always be cheerful, um… know enough to be interesting to him—"

"But not so much that he feels threatened!"

"Oh, no, anything but that. And…That was five, wasn't it?"

"That's it."

"I bet Alek didn't make Emlyn do any of those things."

"I bet Alek couldn't make Emlyn do anything if he tried."

"I bet he didn't try," Ruth said. "He wouldn't."

Adla looked away from Ruth's reflection to give her a moment alone and trimmed a few long hairs over her ear. She pulled the towel off her shoulders when she finished and shook it out over the floor.

Ruth's knee started bouncing. She looked uncertainly at herself. "I've never been out during the day the way you have."

"Don't worry." Adla shaped Ruth's newly short hair. "I'll teach you."

Adla stopped in the doorway to the Larsen's kitchen on her way out and said goodbye to Sabrina, but not before passing on a message from Ruth that she was studying a difficult section and asked not to be disturbed. Sabrina turned from a bowl of cookie dough and smiled over her shoulder. "Thank you, Adla. Please give my regards to your mother."

Holding the door open a fraction of an inch, Adla made sure Reuben wasn't walking down the alley, saw that Ruth's dad was engaged with a customer, and stepped outside. She closed the door quietly and looked up at the roof. Ruth, having also seen that her father was distracted, climbed over the wall and dropped into the alley with the rifle on her back. She quickly took it off and gave it to Adla, and they started in the opposite direction.

"Boys." Stewart's voice was deep, authoritative.

They stopped and turned to face him.

He stepped out of his booth, his dark brown eyes concealed by the day's reflection in his glasses. He beckoned, and they went to him.

"Hi, Papa," Ruth said.

Stewart looked her over carefully but impassively, his thick arms crossed over his chest. He took a long, slow breath, suddenly raising his eyebrows and nodding politely at two men passing by, then bent over and pretended to tie his shoelace while dirtying his hands on the ground. He stood and jovially, but gently, smacked Ruth's cheeks and jaw. "It's about time, lazy boy!" he boomed. "Don't forget to pick up my watch while you're out." He grabbed Adla by the cheeks and smooshed his hands around. "And you," he said, his next words hushed, "keep her safe."

"I can keep myself safe," Ruth said.

Stewart turned to his daughter and straightened her t-shirt's shoulder seams. "Know your limitations, kid," he muttered. "It's not a flaw. She has more experience, so rely on it. Understood?"

"Yes, Papa."

He looked at them both a final time, then stepped back into his booth and busied himself with a stack of blankets.

Ruth touched her face where her dad had left grainy dust.

"How does he know my experience?" Adla whispered.

Ruth shrugged, still tapping at her cheeks.

Adla felt her own face and said, "Good?"

"Manly." Ruth giggled. "Me?"

"Same. Don't smile."

Ruth stopped smiling.

Adla whispered, "Well, now we can't go until you stop looking so scared."

Ruth fixed her face until she passed as more arrogant than frightened, and they started back down the alley. She asked Adla, "Where are we going, anyway?"

"Wherever we might find him."

Adla and Ruth traversed the busy market street, with Adla stealing frequent looks at guards. None seemed to notice her or Ruth. Ruth had been good about taking Adla's advice to keep her shoulders back and, now and then, force herself not to move out of someone's way if they were walking toward her. Every once in a while, Adla said, Ruth had to pretend not to see them and make them move for her.

They reached the end of the busy block. Ruth, though not smiling, still looked too happy. Adla said, "Let's go home. We'll try again tomorrow."

"No! Not yet. Please? It's so fun being out here like this. Can't we keep looking?"

Adla said they could if Ruth stopped taking everything in like a tourist. "Treat it like you've seen it all a hundred times."

They explored the streets and the faces of the guards as nonchalantly as possible until they arrived at the corner of the sport park. Adla stopped to study a small group of cigarette-smoking guards lounging on benches and dwarf walls.

Ruth whispered, "Should we stand here staring at them like this? Even as boys?"

He was there, sitting on a bench with his legs spread impossibly wide, an arm flung over the back, his rifle on his lap. Adla recognized his thin, downturned mouth, his scraggly tan beard, his small eyes.

"Adla," Ruth urged.

A different guard looked over at Adla and Ruth as they started walking away.

"This way," Adla said, leading Ruth down a narrow side street. "Hurry. But not too fast."

They came to an abandoned house situated behind the store that was directly across the street from the park. The house's rooftop was close enough to the store's for them to be able to make the jump. Adla went first through the front door, left unlocked but partially blocked by pillows and dishes and school papers strewn all over the floor. She hurried up the stairs and to the roof without waiting for Ruth, then ran to the edge and leaped across to the neighboring rooftop, performing one of the maneuvers she'd practiced countless times on her own roof: a safety roll with the rifle held to her chest. She crouched behind the parapet, propped her elbows on the ledge, and sighted down the rifle.

She had never practiced what would come next. Only guards could use the range, and only rich people with land had the space to make their own.

"You found Emlyn's guard?" Ruth said.

Adla waved a hand behind her. "Get down."

Ruth got down. "Which one is he?"

"Sh." Adla breathed. Adjusted her grip. Breathed. Squeezed. POP!

She ducked behind the wall. After a couple of seconds, she slowly peered over.

He was still standing, looking around.

"Shit," Adla said, quiet, frantic. "Shit, shit. Shit, shit."

Ruth whispered, "They're all just standing there. Why aren't they hiding?"

"They're morons." Adla swung her weapon back onto the wall, aimed, and shot again. The guard spun, his forearm grazed. Ducking, Adla said, "Shit!"

"*WHERE ARE YOU?*" he screamed.

Ruth said, "Should we feel bad? Are they too stupid to kill?"

"They're smart enough to be cruel." Adla took a deep breath and peeked over the wall. He was looking to his right, but they were directly across from him. She readied the rifle, aimed, and shot, hitting him in the leg. He cried out. The others ran to him.

POP! Her bullet tore Emlyn's guard's shoulder.

POP! That one missed him entirely, passing clear through the head of a guard standing next to him.

"Oh…" Adla said.

The guards' confusion and anger built into an aimless, chaotic frenzy as they ran this way and that way, bumping into each other because they were watching the building and the spreading blood instead of where they were going.

Bracing herself as sturdily as she could and taking careful aim, Adla rapid-fired the rest of her ammunition into Emlyn's murderer, turning his entire chest and one of his arms red and dropping him to the ground. She grimaced at the gore, but a faint, unconscious smile settled into her cheeks.

"Let's go. Adla! They're crossing the street."

Adla strapped on the rifle. Shouting carried up from below. It would take longer to go back through the abandoned house, so they climbed over the wall opposite the side street, dropping into the alley with the metal fence hiding them from pedestrian traffic. They ran.

That night, Adla stepped into the living room while her mother was reading by flashlight on the couch. Blythe lowered her book and shined the light on the rug, making a path for Adla to join her.

Adla sat on the floor where she was and circled her arms around her knees. "I killed someone today. A guard."

Blythe said nothing for several seconds, then asked, "Do you want to talk about it?"

"It—" Adla stopped. She squeezed her knees closer. "No."

"Are you okay?"

"I think so," Adla said. "Yeah. Yeah, I'm okay."

A sudden, guttural sob erupted from Blythe and the flashlight fell to the couch.

"I disappointed you," Adla said.

"No." It was almost unintelligible.

"Would Dad be disappointed?" she said softly.

Blythe managed, "No, Adla. Never." The flashlight went dark. Her involuntary gasps gradually waned, and she cleared her throat. "I had wished that, somehow, you would never have to experience violence first-hand."

Adla tugged at her hair. The window was framed yellow by the light of a streetlamp. They couldn't close the curtains. They'd been open when the guards had come, so they'd had to stay open. Adla said, "I feel like I should...I feel like I'm supposed to want to find a way that doesn't hurt people."

"Don't be ridiculous." Blythe's voice was hard. "The only people who respond to peace are peaceful people. Adla, I don't know what else you have planned, or if you're finished, now, but if there is more...Is there more?"

"I think so." Quietly, "Yeah."

"Yes."

Adla groaned.

Blythe turned on the flashlight and pointed it at her. "Let me be your everyday mother."

"Yes. Yes, mother."

Blythe set the flashlight on the floor, pointing it under the couch to give them just enough light to see each other without making the room look lit from the outside. "I know you think you know what you're doing," she said. "But it can be easy to get carried away. Whatever you have left to do out there, I want you to be patient, and I want you to be smart. Remember the old story of the senator and his loyal assistant any time you're tempted to hurry."

"I don't know the—"

"I'm going to tell you."

In the old story of the senator and his loyal assistant, Blythe said, the loyal assistant was angry when the senator's personal rival, an evangelical political figure, hosted a party on the same night the senator had planned an important event, stealing influential guests and attracting the attention the senator had hoped would boost his campaign. It wasn't uncommon back then to kill people for such things—

"For stealing party guests?"

"It was an unusual time, Adla. People would shoot politicians speaking at outdoor events, threaten to kidnap state representatives…" She went on: During the day, the loyal assistant couldn't get past the rival's ever-present armed entourage, and he certainly couldn't break into his house at night without putting his own life at risk, so killing him was out of the question. But he did still want revenge for the disappointment the senator had suffered. "Because this also took place when men in power still cared about public perception—many could be humiliated into abandoning their post—the loyal assistant ultimately decided to create an 'accidental' private meeting between the rival and—well—a woman."

"So?"

"This very intimate meeting between the *married* evangelical man and the…the professionally tender woman was photographed and leaked to the press, and…Well, I know it means nothing these days, and it's not even a very good story, but—The point, my walnut, is that it took some planning and a little time, but the loyal assistant did get revenge on the senator's rival. He also didn't die, Adla, which is what I'm trying to—"

"I understand."

Adla and Ruth were kneeling at their parapets, their arms crossed and hanging over their respective ledges.

"Well?" Adla said.

"Let me think, I said."

"I only asked what you thought. I'm not asking you to go with—"

The door behind Ruth swung open. Reuben, round-faced and stocky, stepped onto the roof. "Mom wants—"

Adla started to duck behind the wall, but it was too late. He had already seen her, and it was obvious he recognized her after all this time. She rose back up and stayed.

Looking at Adla, Reuben asked Ruth, "What's with your hair?"

"Please, Reuby, don't tell on Ad—"

"So now you look like her." He pointed his chin at Adla. "And like that girl they—Like a boy."

"I don't look like a boy," Ruth said. "I look like a girl with short hair. I'm allowed."

"You shouldn't be. Better wear extra makeup when you go out, little sis, or you'll get your ass kicked."

Adla glared at Reuben. He glared back. Adla didn't look away.

"Reuby, please promise you won't say anything about her being here."

He snorted. "It's been four years. Why would I do it now?"

Adla's scalp turned cold. She said, "How did you know?"

"You and your mom suck with that flashlight. You can see it moving around from outside." He raised his eyebrows. "You know, where it's dark. Anyway, you're lucky I know. If I didn't, you wouldn't be here for real."

"I thought…" Adla said, "I thought you…"

"You're my sister's best friend. She'd be sad if they killed you.—Look, this has been special, but I have better things to do. Shit went down yesterday, and… What the hell am I telling you two for? Help mom with whatever she wants help with," he said to Ruth. "It's your fucking job." He gave his sister a departing look that, for a fraction of a second, was soft. The door closed behind him without slamming.

Adla and Ruth looked at each other, speechless.

"I guess I have to go," Ruth said.

"Wait. I wanted to say and you really have to know that I'm not asking you to go with me, and I don't want you to do anything you don't want to do."

"I know you're not asking, and I'd never do anything unless I wanted to." Ruth wiped dust off her knees. "So? When do we visit Carla?"

"Tonight."

Adla, Ruth, and Carla sat close together on Carla's rumpled couch in a sparsely furnished living room. She didn't have much because she couldn't afford much, she'd explained when they'd looked around for a place to sit. Both of her parents had been bombed by an exploding human two years before, and Neil, the owner of the liquor store she'd lived above with her parents, had agreed to let her stay for free if she stocked the shelves and cleaned for him every day before opening. He gave her some money, but it was only enough for food delivery.

When Adla and Ruth noticed the cell phone on her floor, its narrow black cord plugged into the wall and its battery light glowing green against the antenna hub, Carla said it had been a Christmas present from her parents. "It was the only thing I got that year because it was so expensive, so I have to keep it. Maybe someday I can use it again." It hadn't worked since the first bill had come due after her parents' death.

Adla apologized for what had happened to them, feeling guilty even though her mother didn't make vests, anymore. Had it happened longer than three years ago, her parents could have been responsible. She mentioned none of that to Carla.

"They were reckless," Carla said. "They knew meetings were watched, but they still went to some guy's house." She looked around the room at their own meeting. "No more coming here after this." It was pointless, anyway, she said. As far as she knew, anyone who had plans to change things ended up dead before any changes could be made. Everyone suspected the guards were responsible for the bombings, but no one had proof, and anyway, there was no beating it. "Unless they keep killing each other off. Get themselves out of the way as the first line of defense." She laughed. "Did you hear two of them had some kind of honor duel the other day? They both died. That's what Neil said a guard said."

Ruth told her what had really happened in the sport park.

"That was you?"

"We, um, want to do more," Ruth said. "That's why we're here."

"Since you're Emlyn's cousin, we thought maybe you'd know some of the others she was training," Adla said. "And, well, if you did know them, maybe—We know just because they can do what we can do doesn't mean they also want to kill people, but—"

"I know a few. They won't want to kill people," Carla said, "but they'll want to kill guards. I can think of four right now who will. And I can convince a couple more." Anyone who was sneaking out at night to leap off tall buildings was already looking for some kind of trouble, she said.

Adla said she and Ruth had never seen anyone else out there when they were with Emlyn and Alek.

"Emlyn planned it that way. She thought we'd be too noisy, or something, if we were all out there at once." Carla had met some of the others, but not Adla and Ruth, she explained, because the others lived closer to her, and Carla felt more secure on her own side of town. Emlyn would bring her along now and then to help train. "But I guess I'm about to leave my comfort zone."

Adla asked when they could meet the others.

Carla said, "How's tomorrow night?"

Adla, Ruth, and Carla waited under the olive tree. One by one, girl after girl arrived, some with short hair and others with long hair stuffed into thin knit caps. Carla introduced them as they appeared, going past their names and ages at times to add her own assessments: Josie, who had short hair, was sixteen years old and "unbelievably energetic"; Charlotte, seventeen, also with short hair, was laid-back but quick; Gloria, eighteen and objectively beautiful, had long dark hair that Carla said she could put to good use ("Maybe I can be a distraction," Gloria agreed); Fawn, short hair, seventeen, was, Carla said, "a warrior in spirit"; Taz, nineteen with shoulder-length hair, was short "but a hell of a vaulter, and she sees everything"; Rose, seventeen, was quiet "unless provoked" and had androgynous facial features and short hair; and Sadie, nineteen, had "useless perfect posture," long hair, and little patience.

"That's everyone," Carla said.

When Adla said she thought Fawn, Rose, Josie, Sadie (if she cut her hair), and Carla (if she learned to stiffen her walk) could be boys for daytime operations and the rest should stay girls, there was a confused silence. What did being boys mean? they finally asked. What daytime operations? They only went out at night.

"But your hair," Adla said, indicating those with short hair.

None, it turned out, had cut it for the same reason Adla's hair had always been short. They either hadn't liked the hassle of long hair, or it had been their personal rebellion, but not one had been outside during the day unless accompanied by a male and wearing the required pink. And, of course, heavy makeup as compensation should any men find the hair offensive.

"You just walk around the streets by yourself during the day?" Carla's eyes were wide.

The rest made hushed noises of awe.

"We'll practice," Fawn said. "We can do it."

Minutes later, Gloria was silencing the group by speaking the loudest, which was still not very loud in a meeting whose members were committed to being undiscovered. "For people—For people—Hey! *For people who have never done anything like this before*," she said, "that we're all talking and no one is listening makes me think we're all probably going to die. Will everyone," she commanded as quietly as she could, "please shut up!"

They stopped talking and waited for her to continue.

"I have nothing else to say," she said.

Adla said, "Raise your hand if your parents don't have a gun."

All hands stayed down.

"Raise your hand if there's a rifle in your house." They all raised their hands. "Handguns." All hands went up again. "Raise your hand if you don't know how to use the guns you have."

"My mom taught me," one said.

"Same here."

"My dad showed me."

"Mine, too."

"I said if you don't know how to use them."

Charlotte raised her hand.

"I live close," Gloria said. "I can teach her to point and shoot Deagle."

Charlotte said, "Who's Deagle?"

"Desert Eagle. Deagle." Gloria formed her thumb and finger into a gun. "Bang."

Ruth said, "I guess we should…Well, um, is everyone okay with killing people?"

"Not people. Guards." Carla uncrossed her legs and stretched. "I've been fantasizing about it for years. I see them from my window, coming, going. I've had so many dreams about killing them I'm actually worried it won't feel as good as I think it will."

Everyone else said they were also fine with it.

"But they have training, and there are so many of them," Josie said.

"A lot of them have muscles, so they look like they can fight," Adla said, "but I don't think they actually train at anything, and they can't do what we do." There were small smiles of pride and sadness, and soft murmurs thanking

Emlyn. "And we won't try to get them all at once, anyway, so it doesn't matter that they have more people than we do."

Carla added that the guards also didn't have the benefit of knowing where the girls would be at any given time. But Carla knew enough about the guards' schedules, at least in her part of town, to make it easier to catch them by surprise.

They should start small, Adla said, and reduce the guards' numbers gradually but swiftly. She told them about the error in judgment she'd made when she'd targeted Emlyn's guard, that she'd failed to consider whether the leftover guards would be too much for her and Ruth to handle, "and they were." Easing into things at the beginning by taking down the guards when they were alone, or at least close to it, she said, would allow them to learn as they went.

After everyone agreed that that made sense, planning began.

Blythe lowered thread onto the spool pin of an old treadle machine Sabrina had had Stewart sneak over soon after Abe's death. It had been in Sabrina's family for generations, Stewart had informed her, and, as instructed by Sabrina, he had also emphasized its excellent condition. The only condition Blythe had cared about at the time was that it didn't require electricity, an important factor for the first several months following Adla's and her "abandonment" of the house. Eventually Stewart had had the electricity turned on under his own name so Blythe and Adla could, at the very least, have functioning kitchen appliances even if they never used the lights.

Adla was leaning against the wall, watching her mother turn the machine's handle to wind the thread onto the bobbin. A short stack of shirts sat on the table next to the machine, the stitching standing out from the contrasting color of the fabric.

"I've seen people wearing your clothes," Adla said. "Why do you think they haven't made Stewart make vests like they made Dad?"

"Because I use running stitches, now. I used to backstitch everything. Stewart also buys …well, inexpensive fabric." She pulled back the slide plate and dropped in the bobbin. "How many of you are there?"

"Ten, now. One left a few weeks ago because she was afraid of going out as a man, but she's back."

"And how many are you prepared to lose?" When Adla didn't answer, Blythe nodded. "What happened to Emlyn happened when she wasn't asking for it. You're asking for it, Adla."

That was the key difference, Adla explained. They were going after the guards. Emlyn hadn't been prepared.

"Are you truly prepared?"

Uncertainly, Adla said, "Yes."

Blythe closed the slide plate and threaded the needle. "If I can help you in any way…"

Adla said, "Thank you."

Adla jumped over the alley to Ruth's rooftop with the rifle on her back and gave her the handgun from her belt. Ruth, Adla had learned on their way home from their first meeting with the others, had had no experience with either her father's AR-15 or his antique revolver, but as one of the three people who'd called everyone to the meeting, she hadn't said anything because it would have embarrassed her to be one of the few who didn't know what she was doing. The next day, Adla had started familiarizing her with how the AR-15 and her own Desert Eagle functioned and how to maneuver with them on her person.

Ruth slid the pistol into a canvas holster on her waist. She stared down at it.

"You probably won't have to use it," Adla said. "Today, I mean."

"No?" She looked relieved.

"But you should have it if you need it."

"I'm not scared," she said.

"I didn't think you were."

"Okay."

"Ready?"

Ruth nodded, and they walked along the rooftop parallel to the alley, jumped to the next roof, and kept going until they found a deserted alley to drop into. From there, they made their way to busy Main Street, talking, laughing, and occasionally shoulder-punching each other to stay invisible.

"When you have to acknowledge them with a nod, or something," Adla said, "remember to make it seem like you're doing them a favor."

Two guards and a little boy were standing a short distance from a popular bread booth. Adla muttered to Ruth to pretend to be interested in something or someone to her right so that her face would be turned away. Adla watched the guards as they passed, but they took no notice of her and Ruth. They were absorbed in conversation, glancing occasionally at the bread vendor.

At the tail end of the market block where activity was lighter, they rounded the corner onto a side street and climbed to the top of a bakery. Adla took her shooting position on the parapet, and Ruth stood back to avoid being seen from below.

Across the street, Carla and Rose were already waiting on the rooftop of an electronics store, Carla in position at the parapet and Rose standing a safe distance behind.

Below, the two guards, now without the little boy but occasionally checking on him with glances over their shoulders, wandered from booth to storefront, slowly nearing the bakery and the electronics store.

Carla motioned to Adla. Adla gave a thumbs-up to indicate she had also seen the guards. They waited for them to get closer.

Carla wiped her hand on her pants and returned it to her weapon.

"Are you nervous?" Rose whispered.

"Of course I'm nervous."

"Are they getting close?"

"M-hm."

"How close?"

"Fifty-point-six-four-two feet."

"You don't have to be snotty."

Across the street on the bakery rooftop, Ruth tapped Adla's shoulder. Adla turned to find Ruth just behind her on her hands and knees.

"I want to do it," Ruth said.

"It's not the plan."

"Let me do it. It's not fair to make you do it all the time." It was good that there were only two of them, too, Ruth argued, because she needed to practice just like Adla had needed to practice at the sport park, and this was safer.

There was little time for conversation, so Adla gave her the rifle. "Remember. Carla goes first. You're second. If you can't do it," she said as Ruth looked down the sight, "don't pretend you—"

"You did it," she said in solidarity.

Adla kneeled beside her and waited, watching with her. The guards didn't appear to be speaking to each other. They stopped at a booth, said a few words to the vendor, waited, and moved on.

Finally, they were in the desired range and hadn't once looked at anything higher than second-story windows.

POP!

The guard on the left stopped walking, then dropped.

"You're up, Ruth," Adla reminded her.

On the electronics store rooftop, Carla was backing away from the wall with a thumbs-up to Adla and Ruth. She strapped her rifle over her shoulder and joined Rose.

"Well?" Rose said. "How was it?"

Carla avoided her eyes. She crouched to wait.

On the bakery rooftop, Adla urged, "Ruth. Your turn. Shoot!"

The other guard had his AR-15 aimed at the electronics store's rooftop, but Carla and Rose were standing too far back for him to see them.

Ruth aimed, breathed steadily as she'd been taught, and closed her eyes.

"What are you doing?" Adla whispered.

Ruth opened her eyes. The rifle's sight crossed over the guard's face, lost him, found his arm, and then his chest. His weapon was still up, but he wasn't aiming. He was looking in all directions, the gun held in one spot.

Carla, having not heard the anticipated shot, waved her arms.

Ruth lowered the rifle and backed away from the wall. "I'm sorry. I thought I could."

On top of the electronics store, Carla bear-crawled across the roof on her hands and feet, swung the rifle off her shoulder, aimed at the street—

POP! A bullet from below struck through the wall near Carla's face, blasting a spray of brick and stucco into her eyes.

After a moment of shock, Adla picked up the rifle and braced herself on the wall. The guard was running toward the electronic store's entrance. She fired, but too late. He disappeared inside. PING! The bullet hit the sidewalk where he'd just been. She slung the rifle over her back, waved in the general direction of Carla and Rose to tell them to leave, and yanked at Ruth. "Let's go!"

"I'm sorry."

They ran toward the opposite end of the building to jump off there, their best option for being hidden from the guard when he made it to his rooftop.

"Do you need to go home?" Adla asked Ruth.

"I'm not leaving you. It won't happen again."

On top of the electronics store, Carla was futilely wiping at the blood on her eyes and asking whether they'd gotten them.

Rose, leading her to the door to the stairs, said, "Adla got the other one. We have to go."

Ruth and Adla swung over the bakery rooftop's parapet and dropped into the rear alley. "At least you got him," Ruth said.

"He ran inside too fast."

"You mean he's—Do Carla and Rose know?"

Adla stopped short, realizing her mistake. She had waved at them to leave, assuming they would understand she was telling them to get out of there, but of course there was no way they could know she hadn't killed the guard. "No."

Rose, guiding a blinded Carla, opened the door from the rooftop to the stairs and was suddenly face to face with the guard, his hand out for the doorknob.

He raised his rifle and pointed it at them. "Back." He glanced at Carla's blood-smeared face and closed eyes and dismissed her. Rose he treated with some curiosity. Holding Carla's arm, she guided her backward until he commanded them to stop. He nodded at the handgun on Rose's hip. "Give it to me."

Rose did as she was told.

He set the gun at his feet, stood straight, squared his shoulders, and aimed his rifle at Carla's head.

Adla and Ruth crossed the street toward the electronics store. A gunshot sounded from the roof, and a man's voice bellowed, "Stay put!" Adla pulled Ruth into the store's alley and they crouched behind the business's garbage container. Adla reminded Ruth to be prepared.

Ruth readied the handgun, displaying her grip to assure Adla that her index finger was flat against the barrel and not on the trigger. She whispered, "We have to go up there."

"We can't. What if we make it worse?"

On the store's rooftop, the guard stepped to the side to avoid the blood spreading from Carla's head. He kept his weapon trained on Rose. "Who's helping you?"

"What do you—" She stopped herself. She hadn't lowered her voice to match her clothing, her bound chest. The guard's face hardened, then worked into an unpleasant smile. Because it was possible he would believe a person who looked her age could still be experiencing voice changes, she lowered it and tried again. "What do you mean?"

The guard laughed. "Sure, baby." He laughed again. "A fucking chick." He stopped smiling, then. "How many more?"

"I don't know what you mean."

"How many more of you are there?"

"How many more of us are there…for what?"

"You got a little army?" As he got closer, his boot tapped Carla's calf, making it wobble. "If you don't tell me now, you'll wish you had. Who did the park?"

Rose resisted the reflex to look at the bakery rooftop. "Everyone said it was some kind of duel."

"Smart ass. I can kill you right now. Doesn't matter to me."

"It was—It was just me and—me and her. No one else. We don't even know any other people. We're girls, you know. We don't really get to go out and make friends."

Without losing Rose as a target, the guard used his toe to push Carla's shirt up until her black binding vest was visible. He looked Rose over. "Show me yours." He aimed at her forehead. "I said show me."

She lifted her shirt, then let it fall.

He grunted his approval. "Now, what would make two disgusting animals like you do something as stupid as all this?"

Rose said, "Her cousin was stoned to death."

He shrugged. "And you?"

"I said I'd hide her gun. I had no idea she planned to kill anyone with it.—The first time, anyway."

"The first time. Ah. Ah, I see. Tell me then, you worthless, two-legged toilet, what'd you think she'd do with it?"

"Think? Me, a girl?" She smiled angrily. "Never." She eased out a hip in a caricature of sexual allure and in the breathy voice of a woman-child said, "I would have asked a man what to think, but there weren't any around, so I just said yes."

Ruth and Adla adjusted their positions in the alley to ease the tension on their knees.

Adla said, "I wish we knew what was happening up th—"

"Sh." Ruth had a view of the alley's opening to the street and indicated that Adla should look.

The guard was guiding Rose down the sidewalk with his fingers squeezing her elbow. Rose, scanning the alley, spotted Adla and Ruth peering out and discreetly directed her eyes at the store rooftop. She mouthed *Dead* before turning away and disappearing past a building on the corner.

Adla looked for indications that anyone on the street had noticed them, but everyone was either lost in conversation or heading somewhere with purpose. She tugged Ruth to follow

Rose, then noticed the little boy. He was now standing bizarrely still near the bread booth, just a few feet from a small group of men having a quiet conversation with the vendor over his counter.

"Shouldn't one of us go up for Carla?" Ruth said.

"Okay, I'll follow Rose, and you—" Adla stopped to look again at the little boy. One of his hands was curled into a tight fist. "Wait," she said. "Look."

She and Ruth stepped closer to the boy, who, other than shaking subtly and darting his eyes around, didn't move.

"Ruth," Adla said.

"I see it," she whispered.

Both were staring at a detonator in a hand that looked too small to hold it, the boy's narrow thumb hovering over the button.

They swiftly rushed him, one on either side. Adla wrenched the detonator from his hand as they plucked him up.

"Hey!" he screamed.

Ruth slapped her hand over his mouth. She and Adla used their low voices to chide him, rubbing their knuckles on his head the way big brothers might, and went faster, struggling with his small, writhing body through the side streets. At an intersection, Ruth alerted Adla to a red pickup speeding through. Rose was in the passenger seat.

Stewart came out of his booth when he saw Ruth and Adla turn into the alley, and at his nod that it was safe, they slipped past him and through the side door into Adla's living room.

Ruth held onto the boy and Adla removed his vest, smacking his hand when he reached for the detonator.

"Stop!" he yelled. "Let me go! I'll tell them where you are! They'll come here and they'll shoot you in the neck!"

Blythe ran in from the kitchen. "What is…?" She took the vest Adla held out to her, studying the seams before setting it on the couch. She shook her head at Adla as if to say, *Not one of mine*, though it had been so long since she had made them, and she had made so few, that there was no reason to think they would still be in circulation. She bent over, hands on her knees, to make herself eye-level with the boy. "How old are you?"

"Ten."

"And where are your parents?"

"Dead."

"I see. I'm very sorry to hear that. Do you have a big sister or brother?"

"No."

Blythe told Adla to hide the vest, and Adla took it out of the room. Blythe said to the boy, "You have no one?"

"I have someone. Someone big and important!"

"Sweetheart, did—"

He smacked her cheek hard with his soft, little hand. "Don't call me that!"

Blythe did not flinch, nor did she touch her face where he had managed to make it sting. "What would you like me to call you?"

"Pax."

"All right, Pax. Did that 'someone big and important' try to kill you today?"

That night, Blythe and Adla sat on Adla's bed over a deeply sleeping Pax.

"I think we should have phones," Adla said.

"Phones? Of course you should have phones. How are you only now thinking about them? You're planning a war against these people and you haven't discussed communication?"

Adla admitted that she hadn't done as much thinking as she, or her mother, would have liked. Not only had she not considered phones or how to get them, never mind afford them, she said, but because of her lack of planning, one of the girls was dead. "And another one is—Rose…He took her."

"Oh, Adla." Blythe used her thumb to wipe Adla's eyes dry, then nodded for them to leave Pax. They sat at the kitchen's small wood table. "This is how the hardest learning happens, sometimes, walnut. I'm so sorry." Blythe held up a hand, then, and listened. Adla did, too, but neither of them heard signs of Pax being awake and eavesdropping. To leave no question, Blythe got up, looked down the hallway, then returned to her seat at the table. She whispered, anyway, "If you need phones, you'll have them."

"How?"

"Just find out how many you need, Adla. But, I will say, fewer is better."

"Mom?"

"Yes?"

"Is there still whisky in the cabinet?"

Blythe raised her eyebrows at her daughter.

She just wanted to try it, she said. And her parents had always seemed to enjoy it when they'd desperately needed a break from something terrible. "Besides," she offered, "if I'm old enough for war, I'm old enough for whisky...?"

Blythe slid back her chair and got two tumblers and the bottle. "You absolutely are." She poured them each a glass, with less in Adla's. Adla took a small sip. Her eyes narrowed and her lips flattened into a pained grimace.

"Well?"

Adla, coughing, said, "I like it."

"Don't like it too much, my daughter."

"Don't worry."

A few hours later, Josie, Fawn, Charlotte, Taz, Sadie, Adla, and Ruth were sitting nervously in the dark under the olive tree.

"I understand if you don't want me to come back after what happened today," Ruth said.

Adla added, "Or me."

Sadie picked up an olive from the ground and rolled it away from her. "It was a mistake. That's all."

"You can't quit now," Fawn said.

"I don't want you to go, either," Josie said. "Besides, this isn't about just us and what we want, and there's too much to do for people to start leaving."

Sadie reminded Adla that she'd started to say something earlier that night about possibly knowing where they'd taken Rose, and Adla told them what she remembered overhearing years before from the guards on the street yelling back and forth about a place they called the shack. "But it was so long ago. It might not be anything."

"Like the lodge?" Sadie said.

"Not the lodge," Adla said. "They said they don't like taking girls there."

"Why?"

"Something about—"

"Who cares what they like?" Fawn threw up her hands. "Did they say where the shack was?"

Taz said she thought she might know. There was an old pet store, she said, that no one would ever know was a pet store if not for the big fish decal on a window. She had seen it only once when she'd gotten ahead of Emlyn on one of their few training nights. "It was in this huge lot, and it had all these windows, so I thought it'd be fun to practice climbing up and jumping off, but she caught up to me and took me a different way. She asked didn't I see those lights, and I guess I didn't, but she said there were lights, Taz, and that we should never practice on or go near most buildings with lights on because it just means people are in there."

Asked why she thought the old pet store might be the shack, Taz said she'd gone back once because of Emlyn's reaction to it. The only people going in or out in the hour she'd watched the door were guards, except for the one time she'd seen a girl being pushed inside.

"Are you sure he was pushing her?" Ruth said. "She didn't want to go in?"

Taz shook her head. "She didn't want to."

"That place is down the street from my house," Fawn said. "I've never seen any girls."

"You're lucky," Taz said.

Sadie said, "We'll start planning for the pet place first, then?"

Adla asked who among them had their own cell phone.

Sadie raised her hand, then rolled her eyes at the giggling accusations of "Ooh-la-la!" and "Fancy!"

After the meeting, before parting ways on their own rooftops that night, Adla said she wanted Ruth to please not feel responsible for what had happened to Carla and Rose. "I should have made sure they knew I missed, but I was rushing and…and I wasn't thinking. It was my fault."

"Maybe," Ruth whispered. "But I was the one who should've shot him."

"So shoot him twice next time."

Ruth smiled, almost, and went inside.

Adla took the stairs down to the kitchen slowly. She walked into the living room and found two lumps under a blanket on the couch with a glowing light between them. "Why are you two still up?"

"I'm always up at night," Pax said from under the fabric.

"And now I suppose I will be, too," Blythe's veiled voice said.

"We're playing checkers. Wanna play?"

"No, thanks." Adla sat on the floor. "Hey, Mom, do you remember the day in the hiding place when the guards—"

"Of course."

"They talked about a place where they kept…" Considering Pax, she said, "It was a storage place? For…?"

"Yes, Adla. I remember."

Adla said she was going to try to find that storage place in case they had the roses she was looking for, and to see how many people worked there.

Blythe pulled the blanket off her head and studied what was visible of Adla. "What is this? Why are you telling me this? You never tell me what you're doing."

CLICK! CLICK! CLICK! "King me!"

Blythe tucked her head under the blanket to stack a checker on top of Pax's solitary disc, then came back out.

"Because I'm going alone," Adla said. "I feel like the roses are there because of me, if they even have any, and it's—I just have to not put anyone else in—I only want to worry about myself, this once, and it won't be that…that thorny, anyway. Probably." But if something happened, if she got lost, she said for Pax's ears, she wanted her mother to be able to tell the others where she'd gone.

"But are you sure—"

"Your turn, stupid woman!" Pax's cloaked hand came down swiftly on Blythe's thigh.

Blythe tore the blanket off the boy's head and snatched his hand and jerked his arm. He looked up at her, eyes wide and lips quivering in the flashlight's glow. "That will stop right now," Blythe said, "unless you want me to strap you back into that vest and send you right out the door. Do you understand?"

Pax nodded, his tears spilling over.

The fish on the dark first story window was less obvious than Taz had made it sound. When Adla had gotten the address before they'd all gone home, Taz had said the shack, if that was what it was, would be easy to find even without the building number. Adla wouldn't have seen it. She would have seen the dim light in the top floor windows, however, and she would have remembered what the guards had said about the top floor.

To the right of the old pet store was an abandoned two-story building, and to the left, a wide patch of asphalt space between the store and a gated driveway to law offices. Adla jumped onto a dark, first-story window ledge of the pet store, leaped from there to a rusted air conditioning wall unit, jumped up to a jutting pipe, caught it, and swung off toward one of the dark second story windows. She gripped the ledge, clinging to the outside of the building in a cat grab, and looked in the open window.

Three cots made up as beds filled the small, nearly dark room. Across the hall, two guards were watching TV on a futon couch. Adla pushed off toward the window to her right. She grabbed it and clung there, peering inside another open window at dim hall light falling on a naked, bruised, body on a bare cot. It was a girl, young, but impossible to know her age beyond that she was probably teenager. It wasn't Rose. The hair was too light in color, and a pink caftan was in a heap on the floor. Adla, her fingers and arms burning, watched closely, looking for signs of breathing. The girl's chest lifted slightly and fell. "Hey," Adla whispered, but the girl didn't respond.

A guard already working down his zipper sauntered in from the hallway. Adla ducked down until she could just barely see into the room. Because the faint light behind the guard hid him in a vague silhouette, Adla couldn't make out his face. "Up an' at 'em, future wifey." He let his pants fall to his ankles and started stepping out of them, his shoes still on. "Aw, hell. You *can* cook, can't ya?"

The girl on the cot didn't acknowledge him, or even move, as he approached her.

Adla released her grip and dropped into the alley. After stretching and resting her arms and hands, she slowly and silently explored the full exterior of the building, getting a look inside every window on both floors. No Rose.

With the shack's floorplan and room configurations now in her head, she made her way toward the electronics store to try to see what there was to see on the roof, but too many guards had gathered there and were gesturing at vantage points and circling the building.

The following morning, Blythe, carrying a thick, letter-sized envelope, opened the door to Adla's room.

Adla closed her notebook on pages filled with ink—names alongside skills, an illustration of an attack plan, a phone tree. "I was just thinking about what would happen when we got our phones," Adla said. "What if we called the same people at the same time and no one answered because everyone was already talking? So I made these lists of who each person should—"

"That's good thinking, Adla. Get dressed."

Adla got up without asking why and turned her back to her mother to put on her binder. "Why are you wearing the gray?"

"Because I'm of age."

"That's not what I meant."

Blythe sat on the bed, the envelope on her lap. When Adla was dressed, Blythe gave it to her.

"How much is this?" Adla fingered through the bills.

"Enough for phones." The clothes had been selling well, she said, and she had been saving for a just-in-case.

"This is all your money?" Adla said, handing it back.

Blythe laughed. "Oh, Adla, no." She laughed some more, her eyes watering. "All these years, and that's all you think I've saved? We hardly have any bills, I make most of your clothes, and—" She wiped her eyes. "There's plenty more, walnut, and when you, I, or we need it, it will be there." Blythe stood and examined Adla's face. "You know, you're getting too old to get away with this much longer."

On her way out, with Blythe standing behind her, Adla kneeled at the cracked-open door, slid her hands around on the ground, then dirtied her face, shirt, pants, and neck. She checked the alley for safety, nodded at Stewart, stepped out, and started to close the door.

Blythe blocked it with her foot. "I'm coming with you."

"What? Why?"

She pushed Adla ahead and closed the door behind them. "I have to think it's a good thing that you take your freedom for granted."

The walk to the store was quick, with Blythe having to work to keep up with Adla's long, cocky strides.

"It's been so long since I've been out," Blythe said. "You're very good, Adla."

"Mom. Not so loud."

When the store was in sight, Blythe asked Adla whether they should walk around some more and wait for the guards standing outside to leave, but Adla said they could be there for a long time and that everything would be fine.

As they got closer, Blythe found herself staring at the very tall, narrow-faced guard on the right.

"Mom," Adla whispered. "Keep walk—" Adla saw it, now, too, but pulled her mother forward. "Walking. Keep walking. Go right past him and don't look at him."

He was older and much thinner, but Jared had changed little, otherwise.

Jared and his three companions paid no attention to Blythe and Adla as they passed and entered the store. Blythe dragged Adla to an empty spot in the back by the coolers and, tucked in a corner between soft drinks and bottled dairy, she crossed her arms over her chest and closed her eyes.

Adla reminded her that it had been years since that day Jared had visited their house, so Blythe shouldn't worry that he would remember them and connect them with Abe and the house they were supposed to have abandoned. The only reason Adla remembered his face at all, she said, was that he had scared her, "And you never forget a scary face." But to Jared, Adla had to be one of hundreds of unmemorable children he scared on a weekly basis, "and you," she bumped her mother's shoulder, "were just another worthless whore."

Blythe opened her eyes. They were pink and wet, and they stared at Adla. "Is that funny to you? Is that how you talk out here?"

"No, I—" She whispered, "You have to be quieter, okay? I didn't mean...I thought I was being—I only meant they don't really notice...well, women. Not really. Please don't cry. I'm sorry."

"This isn't about you."

"Well, then," she said quietly, "I swear you don't have to worry, okay? Everything'll be fine. If he recognized us at all, he would have followed us in."

"I'm not scared, Adla." Blythe released a long breath and used her caftan on her eyes.

"Then what—?"

"Please find your phones so we can leave."

Adla glanced over her mother's shoulder, and then at the man behind the counter. She told Blythe she wanted to find a way to get to the roof, first, explaining—because it would keep the conversation short—that "the girl that died died up there."

"Buy the phones first," Blythe advised. "Then ask to use the restroom."

Adla set two prepaid flip phones on the counter. Behind her, Blythe stole looks at Jared through the glass door. The man behind the register rang them up.

"Got a bathroom?" Adla rubbed the front of her pants where a penis would be.

"No. No bathroom. Go at home."

"I saw a sign back there for a bathroom."

"Not for customers."

Adla leaned over the counter. "Listen," she said quietly. "I know this is a weird thing to ask, but could I get a look at your roof?"

The clerk turned, subtly, to peer over his shoulder at the guards outside. He slid the phones into a plastic bag and pushed the bag at Adla.

"Everyone knows about what happened up there," Adla said. "I promised I'd use one of these to get a picture." She held up the bag.

The clerk lowered his eyebrows. "A picture of what?"

Adla shrugged. "Whatever's up there. They just want to see. Maybe there's blood, or something."

"Get off my counter," the clerk said, and when Adla backed away, he said, "Yeah, there's blood. There's also a dead girl. Those f—" He stopped himself. "The poor kid was sixteen, maybe seventeen. What could she've done? Goddamn Insti— Listen here, I'm not letting that little girl be some kind of, what, entertainment? for you and your friends."

Adla apologized. She whispered that the thing was, she actually knew the dead girl. "My sister's friend. She's going crazy thinking she was just left up there, but I didn't want to say anything, in case—"

"I get it." The clerk tipped his head at the guards. "They're here for her. Said the truck's on the way. Tell your sister I'm real sorry for her loss." He raised an eyebrow. "You're still not getting a picture."

The door to the store opened, and Jared and the other guards entered. One of them told the clerk that the truck should be there soon. Jared stayed behind while the other three marched to the back of the store. He clasped his hands in front of him at his waist, his gaze passing disinterestedly over Blythe and Adla.

Adla looked at Blythe to urge her outside, but Blythe's attention was fixed on Jared. The expression on her face was new to Adla. Her mother had never looked like that before.

Jared turned to face Blythe, and she didn't avert her eyes. "Do you know me?" he said.

"Let's go, Ma." Adla took Blythe's elbow. Nodding at Jared, she said, "Sir."

"Hold on a second."

Adla and Blythe knew better than to disobey a guard. They stopped.

The clerk quickly addressed Jared. "You know, I just remembered something about that day." He circled his finger ceilingward. "I'm pretty sure I saw one of them on the street around the time it was going on. I could give someone a description, if it'd help."

Jared eyed Blythe coldly for a long moment, then said it would indeed help and dismissed Blythe and Adla by turning his back to them.

Once outside, while crossing the street, Adla stopped short and said, "Hatred."

"Pardon me?" Blythe pulled her along.

"In there. You were staring at him. Hatred, right?"

"Everyone hates guards, Adla."

"Yeah, but that was…Is he…Did he kill Dad, or someth—"

"Let's not talk about it."

Blythe continued toward the side street, but Adla suddenly stopped them, again, and smacked the side of her head, saying she'd forgotten to buy extra charging cords. "We need them. I swear. Just in case." She tore open one of the phone packages while leading her mother back to the heart of the market street.

Adla parked Blythe at a produce stand and asked the vendor to watch her. Five minutes and that's it, he said. Adla turned on the phone and waited for the battery symbol. It showed half a charge. "Right back," she said as rudely as she could to her mother, and, "Thanks, man," to the vendor.

In the electronics store, Adla slid two charging cords off the display arm and walked them up to the counter, where Jared was still standing guard. Pretending to try to figure out her phone while the clerk rang her up, she flipped it open and, squinting at it, briefly pointed it in Jared's direction and grabbed a picture of his face a fraction of a second before he turned away to tend to the red truck pulling up outside.

Adla had intended to follow her mother's instructions to get as few phones as possible, but it was essential that each person have her own. They wouldn't always necessarily be together. To get them without arousing suspicion, they'd spread out the purchases over the course of a week, with three of the most believably boy-passing girls buying two phones each. Because Rose was gone, they ended up with an extra, but they reasoned that she would need it when—not "if," they decided together—they found her.

All eight girls, sitting under the olive tree and dressed in full black including caps for their hair and thin scarves for their faces, programmed their phone numbers into the phones in their hands, screens dimmed to their lowest brightness. They finished, passed to the left, and started again. In the center of their circle sat a diagram of their attack plan that they'd discussed, adjusted, and studied night after night under the light of Sadie's phone.

"I still don't understand why we're going to that shack to get some strange girl instead of trying to find Rose," Taz said while thumbing buttons.

"Where do you suggest we look?" Sadie said.

"She might not even be there, anymore," Adla said. "They share with guards in other towns, so we could be going for some other girl. But even if there aren't any girls at all when we get there, it's enough to go just for the guards."

The phones passed again.

The stealthy group worked their way through the shadows, around corners, and across rooftops to the old pet store. They stayed hidden and still until the single guard tasked with circling the perimeter went inside, then Adla and Ruth took one side of the building, jumping, swinging, and climbing up to the side-by-side second-floor windows. Adla, clinging to the ledge outside the window of the room where she'd seen the girl, saw that she was still there. She was wearing the caftan, wrinkled and filthy, and sitting on the cot, staring at a far wall. A tea candle was burning on the floor.

The room across the hall was dark, but faint traces of blue light were coming from the left.

Ruth, clinging to the window to Adla's left, scanned what was an empty room but for three cots. Across the hall, three guards were watching a big game hunting show.

Taz, on the ground floor and standing fifteen feet under Ruth, used a flashlight to peer inside a dark, closed window around the corner from the entrance: storage, as Adla had said. Shelves crowded with animal carriers and fishbowls. She turned off the flashlight and crept to the window beneath Adla, this one lit and also closed. A guard standing behind a desk, his back to the window, pounded the surface with his fist and gestured something at a young guard facing Taz with his hands held behind his back. Taz ducked down and bear-crawled to the driveway of the law offices. Ruth and Adla dropped down and followed.

The three joined the others, who had been waiting against a wall in the law offices' shadow, and relayed the information they'd gathered on the numbers and locations of the guards. They confirmed their plan: two on the shack's roof, one on top of the law office and one on top of the abandoned building, Adla and Ruth entering the second floor, Taz taking the first, and Charlotte watching the front door in case anyone ran out who wasn't supposed to.

"The girl is still there," Adla said, "so I'll take her out on Taz and Ruth's signals that the building is clear."

Worried, Charlotte said, "Do you think anyone will come out the front?"

Adla said she didn't know.

They all checked their weapons, looked at each other, and stood there, shifting on their feet.

"Now?" Sadie said restlessly.

Gloria ran around the corner to the back of the law offices and climbed up to the roof.

Charlotte moved closer to the locked driveway gate for a better view of the shack's entrance.

Sadie barreled toward the shack from the rear lot, springing onto the wall foot-first and, using tenuous hand- and footholds to propel her upward, climbing from window ledge to window ledge until she reached the top and could grab onto the parapet and climb over.

Taz took a ground position at the rear corner of the shack, beneath an office window.

Josie ran past her, heading to the abandoned building next door.

Fawn followed Sadie's path to the roof.

Adla started the climb to the girl's window, stopping first at the window on the left to look inside. She gave a thumbs-up to Ruth, waiting below, before continuing to the window to the right. Ruth made her way to the left window and hung there.

From the rooftop of the law offices, Gloria aimed her rifle at one of the three guards watching TV on the second floor.

From the rooftop of the abandoned building, Josie covered the right side of shack.

Still crouched against the wall outside the second-floor window, Adla mimicked a bird call.

Simultaneously:

- POP! Gloria shot once into the TV room. The window crashed. The two guards sitting at the ends of the futon scrambled to the floor. The one in the middle was still, his head hanging forward on his chest.
- Ruth climbed unnoticed into the empty room across the hall.
- Taz aimed into the ground floor office window where there were two to hit. She breathed. POP! Glass shattered against the back of the guard who had, by this time, been sitting rather than standing at his desk. The other guard, who had taken a seat and was smoking a cigarette, saw Taz right before he slid down and out of his chair, shot in the chest.
- Adla climbed into the kidnapped girl's room and said "Sh" before the girl had time to make a sound.

The girl's head lolled to the side. She looked at Adla warily, shrinking into herself. Adla feigned cupping and jiggling one of her flattened breasts and whispered "female" before bending down and blowing out the candle.

The surviving guard in the first-floor office stood flat against the wall next to the window, his rifle at the ready. He scowled at the ceiling light.

Ruth, bunched up and wide-eyed on the cold tile of the empty room and positioned just outside the stream of light from the TV across the hall, aimed at the two unarmed guards scrambling on all fours behind the futon to retrieve their rifles propped against the wall several feet away.

POP! Another shot from Gloria. One of the guards Ruth was watching fell head-first against the wall and slumped on the floor, blood spreading through the back of his shirt.

Adla led the weak, wobbly girl to the door and looked left down the hallway. No Ruth. She told the girl she would be okay, and that her name was Adla. "Femina," the girl muttered almost inaudibly.

Ruth watched the surviving guard scurry backward over glass and out of her field of view into a position that also happened to be outside Gloria's field of view. He pulled the extension cord for the TV out of the wall, startling Ruth and Adla when the room, and the hallway, flickered into darkness. Ruth clutched her weapon tighter.

Fawn took out her phone and dialed Gloria.

"What?" Gloria whispered.

"What's going on? Can you see anything?"

Gloria shrugged at her from across the lot. "It went dark."

"Should I call Ruth?" Fawn said.

"Are you crazy? No." Gloria folded her phone and shoved it in her back pocket.

On the ground, Taz scurried around the corner to the other office window and looked inside. The guard who'd slid out of his chair was still dead. The other was lunging across the room, one arm held straight out in front of him and going for the light switch. Taz lifted her rifle to aim just as the room went dark. She dropped back down.

Adla squinted into the dark hallway while blocking the entrance with her arm to keep Femina back and safe.

With her rifle slung across her back, Taz ran from as far as she'd been able to get from the building toward the broken office window. She vaulted over the ledge and into the office, landing on the desk. The guard shot—POP! POP! POP!—but Taz had already sprung into a front flip off the desk. She bolted through the door.

Having heard the shots downstairs, Adla inched herself and Femina out of the room and into the second-floor hallway. One step. Two.

Taz backed silently down the first-floor hall, away from the office, her rifle pointed at the door. She stopped at the entrance to the storage room and waited.

Ruth heard crunching, grinding glass outside her room on the second floor. It was getting louder, closer. She got into a crawl position and banged into a cot. The metal foot slid on the floor.

POP-POP-POP-POP! Blinding flashes of light from the TV room and sparks on the floor just outside the door.

Ruth, holding the rifle to her chest, used the sound as cover and rolled to the opposite wall.

The guard in his ground-floor office, hiding behind a coat stand, heard the gunfire and aimed toward the door.

Adla shoved Femina back into the room and listened, but no one was moving. After too many seconds of silence, she said, "Ah-cheeeew!" to draw the guard. *If we have to make them move*, Fawn had said at one of their meetings, *they won't be able to resist the sound of a girl. They'll either want to fuck her or kill her.*

From downstairs in her own stiflingly silent hallway, Taz heard the feminine sneeze on the second floor and threw out her own bait, a highly audible, soft, pouty sigh, as if she'd just discovered a boo-boo.

From their rooftops, Gloria and Josie saw through the windows the sudden white light of flashlights, one upstairs and one downstairs.

Simultaneously:

- Taz's flashlight revealed the enraged face of the guard coming at her, rifle at his cheek, finger on the trigger. She opened up on him with her handgun, dotting his chest and stomach with holes.

- The guard from the TV room was standing at the top of the stairs, his flashlight shining down the hall and into Adla's eyes before she had a chance to turn hers on. Ruth shot at him from behind Adla, and Adla dove into the room.

The guard, unscathed by the bullet that whizzed past his ear, ran down the stairs.

"Guard!" Ruth yelled. "Watch the front!"

Taz heard the thudding in the stairwell and tried to catch him before he got out, but he was too fast. He was already busting through the front door by the time she was ready to shoot.

Josie was taking aim from her position on the abandoned building's rooftop when Charlotte, waiting at the gate, fired three shots—POP!POP!POP!—into his body as soon as he exited.

Adla yelled, "Clear?" from the dark room.

Ruth repeated the call, and someone shouted "All clear!" from outside.

Adla and Ruth supported Femina down the hall and to the stairs as fast as the drugged girl could manage. Sadie and Fawn dropped from the roof to the law offices' driveway as Gloria and Josie dropped down from the old pet store. Adla, Ruth, and Femina came out of the building through the front door and hurried around the corner to join the others.

"Who are we missing?" Adla said.

They all looked at each other, their mouths moving with silent role-taking.

"No one," Sadie said.

"They didn't get a single one of us?" Gloria said.

But one guard did almost get away, Adla reminded them. "As well as we did, as lucky as we were, things could have gone wrong just as—"

A door slammed in the distance.

The girls said hasty, hushed goodbyes and scattered into the shadows.

Adla draped a blanket over Femina, curled up on the couch in some of Adla's clothes, and said she would take her home in the morning after breakfast.

"How?"

"I don't know, yet."

Femina fell asleep, and Adla went up to the roof. After some strength training exercises, she started vaulting back and forth over the cement block and was mid-vault when Reuben opened the door to his rooftop. She landed and caught her breath while waiting patiently for him to say something.

"They say there was some kind of freak attack last night." He slid his hands into his shorts pockets. "Some kind of ninja group, they said. There were hundreds of them."

Adla hid a smile.

"There's a stoning tomorrow morning," he went on. "I think you and Ruth might've known her."

Adla shrugged slowly. "Why would we?"

"I don't think you know exactly what you're dealing with."

"Do you mean you?"

His eyebrows twitched in a flicker of what looked like an expression of offense taken. He said, "Ruth's always admired you, you know. She wants to impress you."

"I feel the same about her."

"That girl. Tomorrow? They said her and some other girl were dressed like men." He looked at her, waiting, but Adla only listened. He said, "They used her up. They're done with her, now. That's why they're bringing her back." He tapped his thighs inside his pockets. "She is where she is, and where she'll be, because of you."

Adla swayed slightly, but steadied herself.

"I don't want my sister to be where that girl is," Reuben said.

"She won't. Ever."

"Sure. Yeah, you know, Ruth likes to write things down. I don't know if you knew that. She has this little notebook she thinks she hides. I find everything there. Like about that other girl-man. Shot. Right? It seems—Ruth didn't say so, didn't write it, or anything, but it seems like that was because of you, too." He looked at Adla for a long time, then shook his head and rubbed his face wearily. "I don't want her to get hurt. She's a good person. And yeah, I know, you're probably a good person, too. But she's my sister." He turned and walked to the door.

"What time tomorrow morning?" Adla said to his back.

"Nine."

Adla lay in the dark on her bed, hot tears irritating the side of her face, until self-pity stopped being enough.

She went to the kitchen with her flashlight and snuck a gag-inducing swallow of whiskey before tip-toeing past a sleeping Femina to the hiding spot, where her mother had tucked away Pax's little suicide vest. She left the rifle in its place.

Early the next morning when everyone else was still asleep, Adla, dressed as Addie and carrying a backpack, eased open the door to her mother's room. Blythe was on her side with her face to the wall. Pax was next to her on his back, an arm lying on her neck and a leg tossed over her waist. Adla leaned in and set an envelope addressed to *Mom* on her dresser, whispered, "I love you," and closed the door. She crept past the living room and up to the roof, where she waited until it was time to leave.

A sizeable group of men was gathered at the clearing when Adla arrived. Rose was already on her knees. The loose neckline of an oversized caftan had left some of her chest exposed. Her mouth was cut and her eyes and cheeks were swollen and sickly purple. Someone had shaved or closely cut her hair in patches. Two guards flanked her. There might have been more standing there, had they not killed so many.

Adla studied the faces in the crowd and spotted Reuben. He saw her at the same time and searched over her shoulder. Looking for Ruth. Adla shook her head. He nodded, then noticed Adla's backpack.

Pleadingly, Adla made a point of looking at Rose and then back at Reuben, urging him to help her.

Reuben looked down as if to say *No,* then noticed Adla's fist and the black wire snaking out of it. He looked back at Rose, and then he stepped sideways through the growing crowd without meeting Adla's eyes again, sliding into the spaces between bodies until he and Adla could no longer see each other.

The energy surrounding Adla was impatient, merciless, cold. Sweating and shaking, she inched her way to the front of the circle.

Rose's eyes were so swollen she probably couldn't see anything, but Adla stared hard at her, anyway, willing her to look her way so she could signal to her to get up and run.

She allowed one, two, and then three minutes to pass, knowing the execution event would start promptly at nine.

"One minute," a guard announced.

Rose bowed her head and dropped her shoulders. Surrender. Adla wouldn't be able to get her attention, now.

One step at a time, cautious of drawing interest, Adla backed through the crowd. She did not think of her mother or of Ruth or of what would happen to her or how it might feel. She thought of her father, and she thought of Emlyn, and she thought of Rose. She whispered to herself, "Don't be afraid. This is simply the way things are."

The audience's energy started to shift, anticipation making them shuffle. The guards were taking their positions.

"Order," one of them screamed.

Adla had moved far back to put enough bodies between Rose and herself to keep Rose out of the blast.

She closed her eyes.

She squeezed the detonator, the last thing she would ever hold, and pressed the button with her thumb.

She opened her eyes.

"…here today to witness the honorable vanquishing of a threat to our orderly system of government, our revered Institution of Chivalry, our peaceful way of life."

Men in the audience grumbled and spat. One squawked, "Kill it!"

Adla pressed the button again.

"When Citizen Charles, here, found this… specimen, it was wearing the clothes of a man, impersonating the only hardworking, upstanding, productive members of this community with the intent to deceive us. This must stop. This will stop. Today. Men, remind your women of their critical role as the subservient, and silent, helper. Forcefully, if you must." He smiled, and men in the audience laughed in a cheerful display of camaraderie. "Furthermore—" He looked out at the increasingly anxious crowd. "All right, I had a whole speech prepared, but to be honest, I don't think I want to waste any more words on this subhuman creature."

The men roared, some clapping loudly as if watching a sport.

Adla pressed the button again, and again, forgetting to be inconspicuous.

A male voice shrieked, "Bomb!"

Adla looked up at two wide blue eyes trained on her, the man's mouth a dark, open circle of shock. She pushed the button again, again—

"Dud!" he loudly corrected, reaching for her, and in an instant she was surrounded, her chest being pressed and crushed by the bodies piling on top of hers. Her shoulder was yanked, the bag's handle torn from her arm, her shirt ripped apart at her chest. Something jabbed her side hard, and she heard a crack. A fist slammed into her cheek. There was unintelligible screaming, demands to drag her to the pit.

Everyone, including Rose's guards, was surrounding Adla while, on a side street less than a block away, Rose was struggling against Reuben, his arms trapping hers at her sides as he dragged her farther away from the clearing.

"You can't take me and leave her there," she protested, twisting and pushing at him. "I have to tell the others. They have to come. Gloria is the closest. Take me to the west side."

"I saved you, all right? That's enough."

"*You* saved—?" She laughed at him. "Take me there now," she said, trying to pull her arms free, "or I'll make the guards think we planned this together. If it kills me, I'll make sure they're as disgusted by you as I am and you'll be the next one waiting for rocks to hit your head until you die. Coward."

Reuben released her, glared at her, pulled the caftan down over her back so that her front was less exposed, and took her hand.

While Reuben and Rose were running across town, Ruth was getting her father's revolver from where he always hid it under his mattress. She stuffed it into a backpack with a letter from Adla that Blythe, in her private indoor clothes and her hair still tangled from sleep, had just rushed over along with a weak Femina, who Stewart had been tasked with taking home.

Rose shoved her arms through the backpack straps and ran out of the house, ignoring her father calling after her.

~

A sharp rock pelted Adla's temple. Warm blood trailed through her hair.

It had taken some time for everyone to get settled and rock-ready after the commotion. The men had slowly slid off her and spread apart. The two who had been immediately on top of her had forced her to stand, their faces promptly screwing into expressions of disgust and malice at the sight of her chest binder and the curve of her waist. "Girl! Girl!" they had yelped, and, fighting back those who were trying to get at her again—"She belongs to us all equally!" one of the men holding her had yowled—they had seized her wrists, one to each, and dragged her to the pit, jerking her from side to side as if hoping to tear her in half.

A rock thumped her chest, now bare.

Emlyn had had friendly faces in the crowd. Adla looked for such faces, even Reuben's. Someone familiar, someone standing quiet and still in the deafening and confounding chaos of senseless hysterics.

The guards had said nothing when they'd shoved her to her knees. Not even about Rose's absence. They had simply held Adla down, a tight hand on each of her naked shoulders, while everyone else had picked up their rocks.

Adla's upper arm stung sharp under the impact of a fist-sized stone. It bounced off her and fell in the sand.

Ruth made it to the clearing and elbowed her way to the front. She watched, helpless, as a rock struck Adla's chin. She willed Adla to see her. Another rock made contact, this one pelting Adla's hip. Ruth looked for a place to hide, somewhere with a good shooting position. There was nowhere safe.

Fawn, dressed as a boy, and Sadie, wearing a pink caftan, came up beside Ruth. Rose, also in shorts and a shirt and the marks on her face covered with foundation and dirt, arrived next with Reuben and Gloria.

Adla saw Ruth first, tense and fidgety and worrying at her backpack straps. She would give herself away like that. Adla widened her eyes at her—*Calm down, they'll notice you*—and then saw, standing next to Ruth, Fawn, Sadie, Rose, and—

A man with a rock the size of a softball hurled it at Adla's head. She slumped.

Ruth was sitting silently on Blythe's living room floor. Across from her, Blythe was not sobbing, but stilly crying, her expression stone, her cheeks reflective with tears. They had been sitting this way for half an hour, neither of them having spoken since Ruth had told her about the stoning.

Clearing her throat, Blythe got up and left the room.

Ruth fiddled with red and black game pieces scattered on the rug until Blythe returned and sat across from her. She slid Adla's phone toward her. "She wanted me to give this to you if...If."

Pax ran into the room, the rifle dragging behind him.

"Pax, no," Blythe breathed, reaching out and taking it from him. "How on earth did you find that?"

Early that evening, Ruth lay on her bed holding Adla's phone. She opened it again, again looking for a message she knew wasn't there. She noticed, however, that there was a picture in the photo file. She opened it to a guard's beautiful, blank face and cool eyes.

Over a month had passed since Adla's death. A full moon was hanging over the breezy desert landscape, its light glistening white on the olive trees' dancing leaves. Their thin rattle was the only sound for miles. Curfew had closed the stores and booths and deserted the streets hours before.

But from the half-lit dimness of the small desert town, one silhouetted figure after another, more even than before, made their way carefully, quietly, across the rough and rocky sand and toward the meeting tree.